# THE DARKENING SKY

# THE DARKENING SKY

A NOVEL BY

## ROBERT GLICK

BASED ON THE TRUE STORY
OF PRINCE WILLIAM SESSARAKOO

*Afterword by Professor Nicholas Cheeseman*
*Director, Centre for African Studies, Oxford University*

WOODLAND FREE PRESS

Published by Woodland Free Press, London, England
www.woodland-free-press.com

Printed in the United Kingdom
First Printing, 2015

A CIP catalogue record of this book is available from the British Library.

ISBN: 978-0-9569602-2-1

*To Gordon and Sam,*
*whose fingerprints are on every page.*

## About the Author

Robert Glick, a citizen of the United States and the United Kingdom, was educated in both countries. He has held various positions in public health and in corporate communications—in New York, Paris, New Delhi and London, where he now resides. *The Darkening Sky* is his second novel; his first, *Closer East*, was also published by Woodland Free Press, in 2011.

## *Afterword: The Life and Times of William Ansah Sessarakoo*

Prof. Nicholas Cheeseman is Director of the Centre for African Studies at Oxford University, where he teaches core courses on themes in African history and social sciences. He splits his time at Oxford equally between the Department of Politics & International Relations and African Studies. He serves as the Chair of Examiners for the Centre for African Studies, and is joint editor of the prestigious journal *African Affairs*.

# PART ONE

# *William,*
# *King of the Endless Sky*

*Hold, hold! Barbarians of the fiercest kind!*
*Fear heaven's red light'ning—'tis a prince ye bind.*
*A prince, who no indulgences could hide,*
*They knew, presumptuous! and the gods defy'd.*

From '*The African Prince, When In England*'
William Dodd (1749)

# • CHAPTER 1 •

As soon as the storm subsided, slender beams of moonlight began to puncture the gaps between the ship's hard-worn, wooden slats. Everywhere they cast ribbons of soft color, in hues of pale white and ashen grey.

With the tilt of the ship, the light landed gently for a time on William's shoulders. It cast a column of silhouettes so faint he could scarcely make out the room's dimensions. All he could see was that the dusky rays were bounded by the wall opposite; all he understood was that infinity was being frustrated by blocks of timber and thin, rusty nails. As if in revolt, the light seemed to heave and surge in chorus with the angry winds that jerked the ship forward. And when at last he closed his heavy eyes, he could still see traces of the ethereal moonlight racing defiantly across his blackened field of vision.

By now, less than half-way through his first Atlantic crossing, William Sessarakoo, young prince of the Fante people, had lost track of the number of days since they'd set sail. He had counted the first few. He'd scored each new sunrise and each new sunset against some private, invented measure of quality. But even that cadenced diversion had lost his interest. The days had begun to run into each other, with nothing to distinguish them except the shifting weather and the dwindling tally of birds circling overhead. More than a week had passed in which any land had been sighted. It was possible that more than a month lay ahead before they would reach any land again.

It was just as well he had lost count of the days, for the crossing was likely to take considerably longer than planned. The prevailing winds were proving light, and the ship had been laden with heavier cargo than was customary. There would be many more nights like this one. Untold nights in which he'd be tossed about, his body trembling and his frail nerves tested.

The squall just ending might have been suffered easily by some of the hardier travelers, but William did not count himself among the hardy. He had never before been to sea, but from his earliest days he had spent long moments, whole days, spellbound on the docks that presided over the waterfront of Annamaboe.

He met the slow, deliberate entry of ships into port with great excitement. It was the same for a majestic schooner – with English, Dutch or French flags flying proudly on the main mast – as it was for a simple fishing boat returning with only a day's meager catch. Each one told of adventure, of risk, and every so often of vast rewards. The rich hoards in their hulls were proof enough of that.

Time and again he would climb aboard these newly arrived vessels, accompanying his father on the inspections routinely conducted for local chiefs, before their precious consignments were carried off far into the West African interior. As the lengthy inspections dragged on, William often stole away, peering into the storerooms or the officers' quarters. There he admired the imposing equipment, and especially the latest instruments by which the crew managed to navigate; the compasses, the telescopes and the intricate maps that were frustratingly indecipherable. He'd seen a timepiece so accurate it could measure the precise hour in London, and so better help to plot a course by the stars. To William, it looked only like an inscrutable mess of shiny metal and burnished wood.

Not once, however, did he dream of gaining passage. Not once did he picture himself casting away, of hiding among the cargo or under the sails, only to be discovered when it would be too late to turn back. It never even occurred to him, for there could be no reason, no exploration or enterprise great enough, to pull him away from paradise.

For paradise it undoubtedly was. At least it was for a carefree young man, still a year shy of twenty. He had never needed to seek pleasure or indulgences, as these seemed to seek him out. With so many brothers and sisters on hand, he always had allies with whom to conspire. He never lacked for material comforts either, as the competing European clans wooing his father's favor did so by littering the household with imported delicacies and amusements. By contrast, the watery horizon, with its emptiness and its secrecy, where men's lives were sometimes lost and their treasure forfeited, was not something to be envied; it was something to be feared.

He had often seen huge waves crashing against the shallows. The cracked shells, driftwood and other detritus, washed up forlorn on the beach, were unmistakable testaments of the ocean's unforgiving potency. Yet none of this had prepared him for the thrashing the waves inflicted on this massive ship. The creaky timbered construction, its lean bow designed to barrel through the worst excesses of the surf, only accentuated the pitching movement. The agitation on board was far more alarming than anything he could have imagined from the safety of the shore.

Somehow, the men in the quarters above him didn't seem to mind the stomach-turning rolls. Every one of them had seen conditions far worse than this. Sailors, he knew, were trained to withstand the sea's wrath. Some, he suspected, might just welcome it, as if to test their steeliness or to flaunt it to the others. All night long they kept up their boisterous riot, impervious to the weather and to the officers' feeble shouts for quiet. They sang their ribald songs, played and lost their drinking games until the early hours, until one by one they fell flat from a vigorous swell, or from exhaustion.

Their clamor and their revelry were a solace to William. He knew all of these men, if not by name, then by character. They were well-known strangers to him, as he'd grown up in the shadow of their kind, in the imperious shadow of the English presence on the Gold Coast. He'd been schooled in their language. He'd studied their curious customs so ill-adapted to the climate and to the traditions of his father's land. His father had even given him an English name. So imagining each of them, drinking themselves into a stupor, stumbling around just above his head, brought a kind of consolation and a familiarity of its own.

It was a familiarity he now desperately craved, for William had left behind on those happy shores so much of what he had known, and almost everything he had come to love. Gone was anything that might have been recognizable. Wholly unaware of the world beyond the narrow skies of Annamaboe, he'd never ventured more than a few miles from home, and only then with trepidation. Beyond the wide cluster of villages under his father's command, ahead of the English fortifications and the protected coastline, for him there was nothing save a vast, perilous field of nothingness.

He laid no claim to the curiosity that comes so naturally to other young men. That had long ago been quashed in him by the menacing stories his mother, his father's other wives, and his many brothers told. Stories of feral, mythical beasts that roamed the forest in search of prey. Of bloodcurdling sounds that could frighten the life from anyone imprudent enough to venture out alone. Of men who had gone into the hinterland to hunt, and who themselves had been hunted. He was certain that a good half of these stories were untrue, calculated to keep him from wandering astray, but that still left the other half to ponder, and to dread. He hadn't the slightest idea what lay outside the cosseted borders of his village and of those nearby. He had never thought to leave behind the easy privilege and advantages that his father's wealth and status bestowed on him.

Not yet gone a fortnight, he thought he might ease his present disquiet by dreaming of home. To conjure up the likeness of his adored younger siblings, memories of lazy afternoons spent at play, or the idle hours spent in the harbor watching the never-ending dance of the shipping trade. He wanted to join the crew above, even if it meant taking part in their rough carousing. Most of all, despite the still thumping waves, he wanted to go on deck, to drink in that radiant moonlight.

But William couldn't join the crew. He couldn't go on deck. He couldn't even bring himself to dream. Not simply because he was lying next to more than two hundred other men in sleep as fretful as his own, but because, like these other men, his legs had long since been shackled to the splintery floorboards.

# • CHAPTER 2 •

Interrupted in their chores or in their lessons, attracted by the mounting commotion, one by one the children scurried toward the stately courtyard of the main house. By now, most of the adults had arrived and were seated cross-legged on the straw-covered floor in their regular places, as if by some unwritten rule or strict hierarchical decree. The women sat together, high-spirited and lively. More reserved, the men kept mostly apart, and mostly quiet. As usual, there was no accounting for the youngest children, who refused to sit still, if only for a moment, and only to be counted. Their game-playing and minor scuffles would end soon enough, predictably, in the wrenching of hair or with quick, fitful blows to the head. The adults were powerless to prevent the tears that surely would follow. In truth, they were quite indifferent to it.

Today especially, their interest lay elsewhere, for early this morning the imperial French ship carrying Badu – first-born son of the chief and elder brother to William – had been seen in the pallid light, making its way unhurriedly back to port. They knew the young man would have lavish stories to tell them. They'd be bewitching stories of audacity, of daring and fiery pursuits. He would wield his many keepsakes and raffish reminders of his sojourn in Paris. Not least, he would have plentiful gifts to share.

Once, that is, he managed to arrive on the doorstep. The slow, graceful docking of the ship, then the trek through the village and the long, steep climb to the house, would take some time yet. It would be the final leg of an unparalleled journey that had taken more than a year to complete, and had seen Badu travel a distance far greater than anyone from Annamaboe had ever dared go. Farther than the forests in which the men regularly hunted. Farther even than the remote volcanic islands off the gulf coast where, in their canoes – and in their desperation – they had often been forced to search for fish.

For generations, those deep forests had claimed their share of victims. Men had been lost to roving cackles of spotted hyenas, to hunger, and to kidnapping by rival tribes. The ancient oceanic islands had taken their own fair cut of villagers, as the fishermen's flimsy boats surrendered to the hazards of the jagged black rocks and to the invisible riptides that drew most everything out to sea.

Badu's leaving to such a far-flung land had been marked with great ceremony; his return would need to be marked as a triumph. It was a feat worthy of the spontaneous march forming from the quay, at the front of which walked the tired, slightly bewildered, and immensely gratified young man.

"Give him the flag. Let him wear the flag!" shouted one of the men, grabbing from William's hands the distinctive yellow and black colors of his father's embroidered ensign.

"Give it back! Father wouldn't stand for it. *Badu* can't wear the flag. It's not his right. Only a *chief* can do that."

"Nonsense. Today, he can do as he likes."

"No. No he can't," protested William. "He can hold

it high at the head of your parade, if he wants to. Let him wave it about for everybody to see. That's what it's for. But he can't *wear* it. That would be . . . that would be an insult."

"Don't be absurd. When's your father ever going to be more proud of his family than today? Your brother's so brave. So fearless. He can wear the flag if he wants to. He can dance on top of it, for all I care."

"Father will be so offended. He'll be so . . . he'll be so angry. I hate to think about it, if he finds out."

"Oh look," said the young man, "Look how it becomes him..."

By now, William's protests were in vain. The crowd had already draped their returning hero in the revered fabric. On each of his shoulders, as if by design, rested one of the wide-eyed leopards that framed the coat-of-arms his father had chosen on becoming *omanhene*, a representation of the chief's strength and of his wise judgment. It seemed to suit Badu's build and his disposition impeccably. Down his back, in sharp profile, hung the guardian spirit, a monstrous figure brandishing a fantastically oversized sword. The flag's elaborate fringe dragged clumsily in places along the pitted ground behind him.

"*That's* an impressive thing to see, isn't it?" said the man, admiring the mob's handiwork. "He looks just like the emperor of all Africa," his remarks trailing off as he raced to join the others in their raucous procession toward the chief's compound.

* *

To Badu, the chaotic reception that awaited him at the compound would prove a disappointment. Back in Paris, however, in the gilded offices of the Compagnie du Sénégal, his hosts could not have been more satisfied. If their only objective when dreaming up such a costly extraction to France of a young African boy had been to impress the local chief's clan, then they were poised to exceed their own determined expectations.

For years they had plotted various schemes by which to gain a foothold into the vast potential of this alien country, and to break the local monopoly that the English Royal African Company had established over the extremely lucrative slave trade. If they were to achieve a permanent position, they would need a sizable tract of land on which to build a fort. They would need men to help build and sustain it, and they would need the collaboration of the *omanhene*, Chief Eno Kurentsi, who held the key to it all. If they couldn't bring him around directly, if their pressure and largesse couldn't break the English stranglehold, they could at least attempt to sway influential members of the chief's family. And in this, they appeared to be succeeding.

Badu had been showered in Paris with many gifts; he received even more in the way of flattery, in the hope that, once home, he might extol the virtues of French culture and authority. But not even Voltaire, the celebrated writer to whom the young visitor had been introduced, could have better scripted his return. Act One had been the extravagant convoy that was leading him up the hillside to his father's house. Act Two was the rich banquet scene that was just opening.

It was a scene constructed with enormous energy, from the first sighting of the returning ship. The house had rarely seen such tumult. The women hadn't been given sufficient time to prepare, least of all to plan the intricate dishes that were familiar on such portentous occasions; so they scrambled to assemble a feast as best they could, and with whatever they could, which was nonetheless considerable.

"Get me more jars from the storeroom, quick," shouted Adwoa to no one in particular, above the din that governed the frantic kitchen that was her special province. "And be careful, for goodness sake!"

Piles of earthenware jars had already been overturned in the flurry of activity, emptied of their spices and their sauces, the spent containers jettisoned onto any free surface or strewn across the floor. Not a single pot, not a single implement was spared its call to duty. Wielding those implements, juggling a confusion of provisions, the women worked at a frenetic tempo, only just managing to avoid collisions with each other as they dashed about the house.

"Careful, I said! And you lot," yelled Adwoa to the girls giggling in the corner, "start roasting the taro we've stored up. I think there's also some grouper and sea-bream left from yesterday's catch. And somebody's got to start cracking open these oysters. It's a disaster," she sighed, "a complete disaster."

She controlled her kitchen like a general controls his troops, issuing terse instructions no one had the courage to oppose. Yet despite the surging bedlam, the smell of red peppers and coconut had started to waft through the rooms like a temperate breeze, their familiar fragrance a generous indication that all was proceeding apace. All the while, the measured sound of the drumbeat leading the cortège up the hillside was getting louder and louder.

"Can we help?" asked Seven, the youngest boy, named not because of his position in the pecking order, but because his mother liked the sound of the English word. He peeked in, and spoke on behalf of all the men and boys loafing about outside.

"Well, you can stay the hell out here, for one thing. You're banned from this place. Banned! That's all I need, you all getting in the way."

"Listen, Seven. Listen boys," said another of the wives, more level-headed than her sister-in-arms. "Do us all a favor, and keep to the courtyard. Go makes yourselves useful there. There's plenty still to do. That's where we need your muscle. And where you might be less of, well, let's face it, less in the way."

"What's still to do?" asked a befuddled Seven. "The courtyard's been swept so many times, it's cleaner than I've ever seen it."

"Clean? Is that all you think we need? Look at the state of the decorations, for one. It's appalling. Is *that* the kind of sloppy reception you think your brother will be expecting?"

In fact, in anticipation of this blissful day, the main structure had for several weeks been ornately festooned with garlands of flowers as vibrant as any spring day and strings of carefully crafted beads. Yet in the heat and in the rains long since passed, these had begun to wilt and to fray. Other adornments had been unraveled by the children at play, or chewed at by the noisy colony of fruit bats that claimed the courtyard as their own each night, to the exasperation of the women and to the delight of the boys.

"All this has to be put right," she said. "The wreaths have to be re-fastened. You've got to get more straw to cover the puddles in the floor. Get to it, there's no time to waste."

"But if we *did* have time," added Seven, "we could get more grass for the leaky roof, and maybe even mend the cracked plaster on the bamboo braces."

"That's not what we need today, son," she said. "Not today, of all days. That'll have to wait. Go rouse up the neighbors. Get them to help you boys fix what you can. And hurry to it."

Those neighbors, the other women of the household, the men not out hunting or down at the port with the unloading ship, were all recruited to help. Their excited preparations continued right up to the moment Badu crossed the threshold of the house, to the rapturous welcome he had anticipated, and to the barrage of banal questions he hadn't.

The questions came in rapid succession, as if he were being interrogated by a tribunal. They came most excitedly from his father's wives, eager to satisfy their unbridled interest in all things French. They wanted a scrupulous report on the fabrics and patterns of the Parisians' clothes, the manner in which their houses were organized, and details of the foreigners' ruler and of his consorts. And still the questions came. Barely had Badu time to answer one question before another was breathlessly posed.

"Tell us, son, did you manage to see their queen?" inquired his mother, Adwoa.

"How many storerooms does she have?" asked one of the other, more assertive women.

"How does she prepare the yams?"

"Does she smell of flowers, like the last governor's wife?"

"Sure I saw the queen," he said. "She was . . . yes, I'd say she was very beautiful. Very fair and very beautiful. And she was kind. At least she was to me, that much I can tell you. She seemed interested, genuinely interested in us, too. She asked me all sorts of things about each of you. Silly things, really."

"What kind of silly things?" asked one of the girls.

"Oh, I don't remember. What difference does it make

anyway? And like a lot of the women there, yes, I *guess* she smelled like flowers. I couldn't tell you which ones though, so don't bother asking me."

"That's a shame," said his nearest sister, with an exaggerated quality of disillusionment. "You should've asked her which flowers she wears. I bet it was lilies."

"I'll bet it was roses," said another.

"Oh yes, roses, like the ones they grow in England," said yet another of the girls. "That would suit a queen."

"Don't be ridiculous, they don't have roses in France. It's not hot enough there for them to grow," retorted the eldest girl, with such authority that her pronouncement wasn't questioned, though it was erroneous.

"Well, lilies then. I like the orange ones best. They're like fire!" said the youngest.

Alarmed by the sudden turn in the conversation, control of which he knew he was already at risk of losing, the young man fought fiercely to continue. Only his mother Adwoa managed to steer the women's attention back to her son's lackluster speech.

"And did you think of us, son?"

"Of course I did, Mother! I wouldn't have wanted to stay there. Not one month more in that dismal place. The winter's so cold in France, really, you can't imagine it. I kept thinking my bones would crack. The cold makes your teeth hurt, and the sun doesn't show itself for months and months. But oh," he sighed, with a melodramatic glance skyward, as if dispatching a secret message back to France, "I *will* miss the ladies!"

At this impudence, some of the women laughed. Others just sneered at him. The boys, on the other hand, would have more detailed questions on this particular topic, though it would be more courteous – and doubtless more profitable – to ask them without their mothers and their sisters present.

Sitting comfortably in the immaculate courtyard, he continued to address his remarks chiefly to the women, not least since his uncles and brothers, covetous of the treatment he was being given, contrived to feign disinterest. It wasn't a posture they could sustain for long. They were as hungry as the others to hear his wondrous tales. He invited some of the children to sit on his knee and in a tight group around him, playfully tousling their hair and bathing them in the attention he knew they wanted. And when, after the shadows had lengthened across much of the cloistered yard, his father at last entered, he bowed deeply and reverently before him.

Chief Kurentsi took his seat on the resplendent, wood-cut stool that served as a potent symbol of his supremacy, as it had for every Fante ruler before him. He sat slightly but noticeably apart from the others. It was a purposeful distance that was not quite detached, but not quite connected either. His demeanor bore the unwavering hallmark of his reign – a dignified, venerable air of indifference – that risked tempering the joyous mood of any celebration, at least until his pipe was lit. Until he was shrouded in its beloved honey-scented smoke, and would give an almost imperceptible wave to signal his assent. Something that, happily, was quick to come this afternoon.

That remoteness, the uneasy chill that seemed forever to emanate from the chief, was all too familiar to his family, and all too feared by his subjects. Rarely did he exhibit anything that might be confused with real emotion. To him, a strong-willed stoicism was the essential guarantor of impartiality. In the bloodthirsty position he had assumed, it was also the guarantor of longevity. Thorny disputes were mediated, weighty contracts arranged, the myriad daily affairs administered, and not once did he succumb to sentiment, as a weaker man might have done. "Your daughter will marry the miller's son," he'd exclaim, without as much as a moment's concern for the weeping girl's thwarted wishes. "Half of your harvest will be paid as damages," he'd say in judgment, undisturbed if it meant ruin or disgrace to an unsuccessful defendant. "My third wife will come tonight to my bed chamber," he'd declare, before changing his mind again, without burdening himself with the raft of practicalities that had to be set in motion to accommodate his whim. Such dispassion, he knew, was necessary for any successful leader; for one who dealt so heavily in the traffic of human slaves, who pitilessly negotiated their sale with a corps of unscrupulous intermediaries, it was indispensable.

This afternoon, too, he sat with a frozen stare, even as those around him gaped in awe as, one after another, Badu unveiled the gifts in his possession. "Good," he would say from time to time, when shown a particularly splendid item, "that will do," even if the family knew, or suspected, that he was for once genuinely impressed. He paused for just a moment longer than was required to examine and to admire the objects. There might even have been the trace of a smile, though it passed so quickly, no one could be certain.

What was clear, however, was that within Badu's trove there was plenty to admire. There was a large-caliber flintlock musket, lighter than any of the other guns in the chief's arsenal, yet just as capable, and just as lethal. A pair of reed-stem pipes, one made of white porcelain and one of ivory, had been ornately sculpted, and were accompanied by several cases of fine, cured tobacco from the West Indies. The colonies offered up their sugar as well, tendered in heavy drums specially prepared on the plantations of Saint-Domingue. There were yards and yards of delicate lace, thick horse tails, a handsome musical instrument that none would ever play, and a conch shell with the chief's initials and the Christian year "1743" outlined in miniature gemstones that, his benefactors should have realized, he was unable to read. For Badu's sisters there were picture books depicting idealized scenes of pastoral life in France. For William, there was a long hunting knife and its sheath of coarse linen, and a pair of leather-trimmed binoculars.

"And in here? What have you hidden from me in here?" asked the chief brusquely, pointing with his walking stick to the crates stacked high on the side.

"They're not hidden, Father. I wanted to keep this surprise for last."

"Show me then. Open these crates before me, or I'll smash them open myself."

"This, Father," he continued "is a kind of alcohol. What the French call cognac. It's like the rum they send you from London, only finer," taking a decoratively-labeled bottle of Armagnac and one of Calvados in each of his hands. "They sent me to the south of their country so I could see where they make it, and *how* they make it. It comes from the juice of cherries and peaches, raspberries and apples. All of this sits in huge copper pots and barrels made of oak, Father, sometimes for years and years. Some, they told me, are older than me. And that's what makes them taste . . ."

"Bah. I'll decide how they taste!" shot back the chief, bored already of his son's tiresome lecture.

Accustomed to the rum supplied by the English, he had taken to consuming so much of this brew that it had begun to consume him, slowly diminishing his legendary faculties. This drink, however, was something entirely different.

It was a revelation. And before long, the chief had a bottle opened from every crate, savoring a taste from each.

"This, son, I will keep. Take these hideous pipes and dreadful shells away. But bring me more of this . . . what's it called?"

"Cognac in their language, Father. Brandy to the English."

"Well, whatever it's called, I don't care. I call it . . . I call it good."

Emboldened, and as if to underscore his great learning, Badu continued his homily. He tried, without much success, to get the chief to admire the different shades of orange and red and browns, to find in them a clue of the fruits from which the brandies were made. He had even less success with the scents – the nuts and the cocoa – which he had intended to set off by gently warming the liquid over the open fire, as the French had instructed him to do. But when he did so, he brought it close to a boil, letting off the vapor and unleashing a stifling aroma that almost choked those closest to the flame.

All this subtlety was well lost on the chief, yet the more of this elixir he drank, the more enchanted of it he became. Inebriation only stiffened his already healthy sense of vigor, and a conviction that he must be the most sought after and the most fortunate of chiefs in all of Africa. He didn't know, he couldn't know, that the French were plying local rulers up and down the Gold Coast with the same gifts, and that they had equivalent designs on their lands as well.

As Badu watched his father enjoy the brandy, as he saw the formality and aloofness slowly melt away, he was pleased. He knew he had done well, and that the mission on which he'd been sent, the risks and the anguish of separation he'd endured, had not been for nothing. He was persuaded that his education abroad had been well-earned and well-received.

His father, even intoxicated, knew better. His private intention had never been as forthright as Badu assumed. It was not as he'd claimed, to obtain tuition for his eldest son in the ways of the merchant trade. Nor was it an excuse for his presumptive heir to relish the debauchery of a foreign capital or the obsequiousness of far-away royal heads, whom he considered his equal, when he considered them at all. Badu had been sent only as a vehicle to transport back the unrestrained bribery on which the chief's fortune relied. A fortune that was critical to his endurance in power. This was influence-peddling in its most raw form, an art in which the chief had become a highly-skilled practitioner. He would wring from the French the maximum benefit he could, in unashamed opposition to the English endowment he had already secured. His eldest son had been put forward as the perfect foil. But that didn't make the gemstones in Badu's custody any less brilliant, the cloth any less luxuriant, or the brandy any less sweet.

## CHAPTER 3

"I trust, William, everything's in place for the ceremony?" asked the chief, eager that the traditional offering of thanks to the spirits be undertaken with appropriate haste.

"Yes, Father, I think so."

"Don't think. For once, just do it."

Adwoa, seated closest to the chief, and recognized as the unquestioned authority on domestic matters, mercifully chimed in.

"Everything *is* in place," she said. "The children are ready. We've washed them from head to toe. We've prepared your costume, and we've readied the gifts for the gods."

Only part of this report was true. The children might have been cleaned, but they were far from ready. They never quite were. As usual, she knew the family would shortly head off to the shrine with many of the youngest still disheveled and disordered. Out of her husband's earshot, she yelled at the most rambunctious of them to settle down and to organize themselves for an imminent departure, but they were loath to be pulled away from their games. The silk wrapping and chips of mulberry bark that emerged in impossible quantities from the crates were far too inviting, and they continued to fashion makeshift headdresses and skirts from them until their mothers pulled them away.

"Would you like to inspect the offerings, Father?" asked William, in a renewed attempt to win even a small sign of the chief's consideration.

"No, I would *not* care to inspect them," he replied sternly. "Stop wasting my time, William. Do you think I'm interested in this kind of detail? Do you not think I might have quite enough to deal with without having to worry about the state of the children or whether the gifts being prepared are adequate?"

"Of course, Father, I'm sorry. I just thought . . ."

"You just thought! Bah! Go and make sure your brother is well cared for. How about I just *assume* everything will be done in time, and to my satisfaction?"

"Very good, Father," replied William, with his head all but in his hands, as he backed away.

Within moments, the march that earlier had led Badu to the house re-formed and headed off in the direction of the shrine, the singing of cheerful tunes as uproarious as before. The children ran ahead, as if being out in front conferred on them some kind of privilege only they could know. They announced the coming of the assembly in their shrill shouts and at full volume, though no such announcement was required, as the regular pounding of the drums could be heard well down the hillside, and for miles around. Soon enough, the whole of the chief's people, men and women by the dozens, were joining the pageant.

The children nevertheless proved useful. They cleared a path on the dirt trail as they advanced, their flat feet kicking up profuse quantities of the parched earth, as if pulling a chalky curtain behind them. They never strayed too far ahead, since even at a tender age they knew the dangers of walking alone or in small numbers, vulnerable to capture by forces they did not yet understand. So they kept in front, but at a safe distance, where they could be watched, and where they could be protected.

As the marchers reached the perimeter of the sacred grove, the character of the congregation instantly transformed. A whispered tone suddenly prevailed, as if one could communicate with the ancestral spirits only in hushed accents. The land itself reflected this altered state. The web of arid trails yielded to dense, ebullient vegetation, where all imported sounds were suffocated. Willowy leaves of plantain pointed the way in. The grasses en route to the grove had mostly been peeled back to make way for farming; here, they were unfettered and untamed, and gave refuge to all manner of life. In the scrub and under the protection of the huge, rutted rock formation, the herons, painted snipes and magpies held sway over an ecosystem whose equilibrium had been unchanged and unchallenged for millennia. The air itself seemed cooler and calmer, as if it had rarely been roused.

The villagers had been coming to the sacred grove, and to the hallowed altar it sheltered, for generations. It was a place for thanksgiving and a place for prayer. An anointed retreat in which to ask for forgiveness, and at times to ask for explanation, but invariably one of profound veneration. They made the journey when the rains didn't come, or when the irate sea refused to give up its stock of fish, but they also came in times of great happiness and achievement, as was today's marking of Badu's return.

For the ceremony to begin, the ancestors would need to be coaxed from their placid slumber. As always, Chief Kurentsi was given the honor of this task. It was both his prerogative and his pleasure.

"Children of the night, awaken," he chanted, again and again, as if prodding a dreaming toddler from a restful sleep. "The faithful summon you. Awaken!"

In the chief's mighty voice, this seemed more like a command than a plea.

"Children of the night, awaken," repeated the crowd, by rote, as one might recite a well-known Bible verse in the recently constructed Anglican church in Annamaboe, a place not one of them had ever presumed to enter.

This chant was the recognized sign for the group to begin communicating directly with their forbearers, led by the priests in songs that were already ancient when their fathers' fathers were still young. They were songs that were meant to soothe the ageless forces, and that filled the atmosphere with passion and with joyfulness.

They would be appeased as well by the offerings of their brood, and not least by the chief's gift, which was to be presented first. He took a handful of gold dust from the leather pouch on his belt – residue of the vast nearby fields at Bambuhu that had nearly been depleted – and sprinkled it atop the simple memorials that dotted the grounds. It was a token to the oracle, and to all the august spirits that dwelled in this consecrated site. Prostrating himself, he issued a single muted prayer of gratitude that none but he could hear, before ceding the stage to the priests, whom he mistrusted, and then to his wife Eukobah, whom he adored.

She was not his first wife. She was not his most valuable wife either, in that she came to the marriage with little dowry and with no appreciable legacy, though one of many daughters of the king of Aquamboo. She was, nevertheless, his favorite. Mother to William, friend and guide to all the children, Eukobah was the winsome woman that every girl wanted to be, and that every boy hoped to find. Affectionate. Kind. With deep-set, cherry-black eyes and pronounced lips that bore an almost immutable smile, her warmth and affability were the supreme antidote to the chief's coolness. He drew often on that warmth, to help keep harmony in the family and to keep peace in his own toughened heart.

An elegant woman, she hadn't been chosen as a wife because of her uncommon beauty. She boasted no more and no less of the alluring physical traits – the thin eyebrows, thick shoulder-length hair, a firm build – that were typical of the women of her tribe. Neither had the elders put her name forward because of her youth; on the day of her wedding, at the age of nineteen, she was among the oldest of his brides. It was, however, her resilience that marked her out. Where so many of her tribe had faltered, she had survived the pestilence, and many other maladies that hadn't a name, unscathed. In the arduous eastern lands from where her people came, she had endured repeated bouts of famine and drought, without complaint and without remonstration. To be tested so, and never to be defeated, was a transcendent sign. The torrent of trials to which she'd been subjected could only be understood as contests from the gods; her monumental fortitude could only be taken as evidence of their approbation, and therefore as a prized asset to be welcomed into any great house. With the clear favor of the deities, Eukobah was petitioned from the earliest days to play a significant role in the spiritual life of her new home, to maintain the pious discipline which she had been taught, and to ensure her family didn't divert from the path of equanimity she had taught herself.

With the crowd watching intently, she walked slowly around the site, pivoting on her heels at irregular intervals to retrace her steps. As she moved, not once did she cast an eye to the ground. Rather, she stared at indeterminate, fixed points in the far distance from which she seemed to take direction. Meanwhile, the pack closed in, pressing her steadily toward the center, hemming her in to a tighter and tighter circle.

Treading on the hard ground, striding over the high drift of fallen leaves, her movements weren't silent. They weren't intended to be. On the contrary, she exaggerated her steps, ensuring that each one let off enough blusterous energy that it would not only rustle up the lifeless foliage, but that it would stir the tentative, wary spirits as well. It was an energy amplified by the spirited waving of her arms and the swaying of her body, bending herself like the branches of a tree in an advancing storm.

"Oh greedy earth," she said, in words – like those of the chief – rehearsed and repeated countless times, "I give you this holy water," drizzling it onto the ground, emptying the clay pots that had been brought to the site for this purpose. "Accept this excellent gift and be satisfied. Let each of us testify to your power, and pledge to you our devotion."

Each of the assembled was then called on to take a sip of the blessed water, as slowly each person recited a very personal oath. She knew the fearsome sanctity of this oath, as did each of them. They knew they invited injury or even death upon themselves if they spoke falsely or didn't follow through on a promise there made. She knew as well that the pledge was directed as much to the ancestors as it was to her husband, the chief, whose power in the temporal world was no less commanding than was that of the oracle in the spiritual realm.

* *

Eukobah wiped the dust from her hands, and rejoined the other women.

"Was he pleased?" she asked of Adwoa. "I wasn't too muddled or too slow?"

"Of course not, dear, the whole service was a great success, from start to finish," she replied, taking her friend's hand in reassurance. "I even caught Eno grinning with pleasure at one point. And why shouldn't he have, it all went so well."

"That's a relief, then. Thank you. Hopefully then I can enjoy the rest of the festivities, with you and the others."

"Yes, come sit with me. You can tell me what you thought of my dear son Badu's performance. He was so nervous, I thought he might burst! I had to bite my lip to stop from laughing."

"Yes, the poor boy," said Eukobah. "He was so agitated."

"All this interest, all this praise. It's not something he's used to. He wants so much to please his father, but . . ."

"But there's risk in it? For sure. Stealing the attention away from his father. I can't say I envy the boy."

"And he knows," said Adwoa, "that one day all this will be *his* responsibility. You and I both know, he's more than a little terrified at the prospect."

"Still, he managed to endure his ordeal in France. That's something, for sure. I don't know how he survived such a thing. To stay away from us for so long, so very far away. I don't think I could have done it."

"Well of course you could have! Just look at what you've done here today. You kept every one of us in line. The French would be no match for you!"

Eukobah had indeed led the service well. But she had been so completely engrossed in the conduct of her religious duties, so stirred by the mesmeric power of the familiar sacraments, that she hadn't noticed her own son's absence from the event. She hadn't remarked that, all day, William had been detached, immune to his older brother's stories, and missing by this time from the frenzied merriment.

Not that this was unusual. He was often absent, and even more often absentminded, quickly sidetracked by a host of petty concerns. He was troubled by his studies, which at his father's insistence had continued well beyond convention, and that seldom held his attention for long. He was troubled too by the coquettish girls around him, who held it always. He was exhausted by the strenuous preparations for today's amusements, and driven to distraction by the reverberations of the day's incessant drumming.

Yet William was more than uninterested; he was unimpressed. Badu's lauded journey to Europe, and his safe return a year later, didn't seem to him the attainment of some high pursuit or victory in some valorous test. His brother hadn't captured a seven-headed river snake or scaled the slippery cliff sides of Mount Afadjato. Where was the honor, where was the risk, in being coddled as the passenger on a foreign ship, or pampered as the guest of a doting king? Begrudgingly, he would grant that these deeds were not commonplace, and that the gifts Badu had in tow were dazzling. Still, they were not quite efforts that history would record with hyperbole or with grand storytelling. Mostly, he thought his brother slightly misguided, and more than a little foolish, for agreeing to leave their perfect home in the first place.

\* \*

That afternoon, William wanted only to return to his cheery routine. To lie down in a verdant field, deciphering the shapes and patterns in the display of gusty clouds cluttered overhead. To guess the number of chambers hidden under a particular ant hill, or to consider the implausible number of minute creatures it would have taken to build these miraculous structures. To do practically anything except sit through yet another hallucinogenic incantation or monotonous ritual, especially one that had his witless brother as the object of its adoration.

More gratifying still would be to abscond with his cousin and friend Kwame, to sit by the docks, watching the enthralling cavalcade of ships entering port. To fish or swim or to see how long they could go without really doing anything at all.

"William, what do you wish for?" asked Kwame, as the pair drew outlines of themselves in the soft sand of Bogi Cove to which they had slipped away, a sanctuary of gentle breezes and secret hideouts accessible only to those brave enough to fight the biting currents and the convulsive surf that protected it.

"What do you mean, what do I wish for? When?"

"I mean, usually. Like now. When you're just, you know, when you're just . . . thinking."

"Oh, I don't know. Nothing really."

"Nothing? Me, I can't help but wish for things. Lots of things! I wish for a whole *pile* of gold. Stacks and stacks of it. And . . . and, I'd like to live in a house up in a tree somewhere. A tree like that one," he said, pointing to the tilting oil palm on the edge of the dune. "I wish I had binoculars, too, like the ones your brother gave you today. And I wish I were stronger. Strong as an elephant! As strong as you are, William," he said, envious of the four years' maturity his friend had on him.

"You might be, one day. Just give it time. And when

you're as big as me, we'll build you a house in a tree, to live in."

"Do you mean it?"

"Of course I mean it, Kwame. We'll build you a house."

"Swear it!"

"I never swear."

"Swear it!" hollered Kwame.

"Never!" replied William, wrestling his younger friend until he was face down in the sand, peppering him with pretend jabs until they both collapsed from laughter.

"I wish . . ."

"What, there's more?"

"I wish we could fly."

"Fly? What, like those gulls?"

"Yes, exactly like those gulls," said Kwame. "You and me. I wish we could fly way out to sea. Far away from here. We could go together, the two of us. Nobody would even miss us. Nobody would even notice we'd gone."

In fact, the young men were often gone. They were habitually truant. It was a chronic act of protest. They were all too frequently absent when chores were assigned in their homes. Inseparable, they often skipped their classes, though their schoolmasters, intent on satisfying the chief, were indisposed to relay reports of their insolence. Today had proved no different. Overlooked in the tizzy of the day's events, the pair had slipped effortlessly away, toward the shelter of the secluded cove.

"I don't mean we'd go for a day," continued Kwame, "or that we'd miss just a couple of lessons. I mean, we should *leave* this place. Forever. We can just collect our sandals, get our knives and things, and leave. Never come back."

"Leave it? You must be crazy. What for?"

"For adventure!"

"Kwame, you're all of fourteen years old."

"Fifteen."

"You're fourteen. What kind of adventure do you expect you'd have? Like the ones you've read about in their English books? That you'd slay a dragon, or meet a beautiful princess? I don't think it would happen like that. That's just the stuff of fairytales. We'd be attacked by wildebeest before sunset. Well, you would be anyway."

"You can say what you want, I'd like to go just the same. To see it for myself."

"To go where?"

"Well, I don't know. To wherever those birds come from. To wherever those ships come from. To the capital, maybe. Or to France!"

"That's absurd. You've never been farther than . . . farther than here, really. Than this beach. Me either. That seems quite far enough away for me already."

"Alright, maybe not France. You pick the place, William. I don't care, just as long as we both go there."

It wasn't surprising that Kwame would trust his friend to choose the destination of any evasion. The location was immaterial. The only thing that mattered to the younger boy was that they travel together.

To Kwame, this friendship with his closest cousin was everything. He thought of William not simply as a friend; other friends could be found. But friends could be forgotten, or they could be forsaken. No, William was more than that. Much more. He was a confidant. An accomplice. Time spent with him, the attention William showered on him, was like a rare and exclusive gift. Not least, it was time spent away from his own family, particularly his father – long-estranged brother to the chief – whose frightful temper was often aimed in Kwame's direction. His cracked nose and puffy eyelids were more than enough testimony to that brutality. Little wonder then that he craved spending time away, in the company of his admired friend. Little wonder, either, that he dreamed of leaving.

Annamaboe held not even the slightest appeal to Kwame. Because the brutish and jealous chief had stripped his father of any power, the family was left without status, and had conferred little ambition on their only son. Not that ambition would have served him much purpose. Only a very slim pathway had been traced for him. Like his father, a consummate hunter, soon he'd be expected to excel at the hunt. He would marry a simple girl of the chief's choosing, and start a family of his own. He would be counted on to feed his family, to help protect the tribe and to keep their timeworn traditions alive. But for a timid, unsettled fourteen-year-old, there was little else to which he could aspire. Above all, he feared he might inherit his father's manner. That he would repeat the pattern, and find himself abject and despised as an adult, and capable of the same blunt cruelty to which he was continually subject. He worried that this cruelty too was preordained.

William too knew that the same blessings of establishing a family would be his. But although he couldn't yet define it, he wanted more, to find his own path, and one that would distinguish him from the exalted brother in whose wake he remained.

As the second son of the chief, achieving that distinctive identity for himself was never going to be easy. For most, it would have seemed superfluous. Everything had come so easily to him. Except for his negligent father, his large family was unflagging in its affection. The physical conditions of their household were unmatched and unfaltering. The fawning English even called him prince. Yet he had never managed to stake out a discrete patch where his unique voice could be heard. And he'd never managed to capture much, if any, of his father's already sparse kindnesses. It was something he would eagerly have accepted in exchange for all the gifts from France his brother could possibly convey.

\* \*

The canoe William and Kwame had taken to Bogi Cove, delivered of their own backbreaking efforts, was embarking today on its maiden voyage. Both had expressed great confidence in the ability of the boat they'd constructed to weather any challenge the capricious sea could throw at it. In private, each had harbored a tinge of misgiving, but this only heightened the exhilaration of the expedition.

They struggled to drag the unwieldy canoe out from under the bramble where they'd moored it and through the hot sands toward the shore. They'd spent incalculable hours building it, hollowing out the shell from a single log of teak, in the same way it had been done for a thousand years. With knives that had dulled from onerous exertion, they painstakingly removed the brittle bark, then smoothed out just enough room for each of them to sit easily, or at least to sit snugly, without fear that the canoe would tip at the first swell. The sharp ends at the front and back would help to cut through those swells, in a simple design the older men had shown them. They had neither the patience nor interest, however, to carve out the ornamentation that would be expected of the more expert men. In their haste to see it completed, neither did they manage to fasten all of the ribs properly to the frame, in a manner that could withstand the worst of the elements. No matter, the craft was buoyant.

She was nimble and she was sturdy. She was a product of their resourcefulness and of their own lacerated hands. It would carry them safely to the cove, so even without those embellishments, it was to be treasured.

The storm clouds that earlier menaced their excursion had thought better of it, and had cleared away. The winds were light and favorable. And if the boys knew the skies well, they knew the sea even better. After all the time they had spent at play in its bounding surf, it had become a companion, whose complexion and character they could anticipate. They had, therefore, rightly forecast a prosaic journey, though they could only express disappointment in the ocean's quiet composure. There was little thrill in that. She had produced few colossal waves on which to prove their prowess or that of their new canoe, and the waves were their field of glory. Held aloft atop a rippling curl, for a moment or two they saw themselves as unopposed rulers, as masters of all they surveyed, only to be brought low again in an instant by the remorseless sea-bed. These were the shortest reigns the continent had ever seen, but full of majesty and delirium while they lasted. True, the ocean showed itself magnanimous enough to allow their ascendancy over and over again, although always with the same lamentable conclusion.

Today's calm seas meant William and Kwame could explore the depths of the littoral caves, carved into the rocky cliffs, without risk. They swam into cavities whose entrance had been enshrouded by layers of moss and plants so abundant as to be almost inviolable. Once inside, through the snarled vegetation and rock, they didn't hesitate to take possession of the chambers, in a solemn ceremony of their own invention.

"I crown you King of the Infinite Seas," said William,

placing a splintered shell, recovered from the ocean floor, on his friend's dripping head.

"I crown you . . . King of the Endless Sky," said Kwame, choosing the remains of a broken shell of even greater size.

"Excellent. I feel stronger already. And taller. Do I look taller to you?"

"Ten feet tall, Your Majesty," said Kwame. "Ten feet."

"As I thought. You look impressive, too, Your Highness. Your people must be so proud of you."

"Ah yes, my people," said the younger friend. "I must be a fair king to them. A good king. And my people will love me because of it."

"No doubt."

"No doubt!"

Walking to the edge of the rock face, William cupped his hands closely and shouted, "Coo, coo..."

"What are you doing? Why are you making that awful noise?"

"We need witnesses. Otherwise, it doesn't count. You want this to be official, don't you?"

"I guess so."

"Of course you do! I'm inviting the birds to come and observe our service. They've been hovering over our heads all day, just waiting for an invitation. Coo, coo," he repeated.

But his calls sounded more like the cry of an injured jackal than the whistle of any bird, and only served to scare them away. In any event, their riotous laughter had long since put off the birds.

"We don't need witnesses. We don't need *anyone*, William. It's just you and me – the King of the Infinite Seas and the King of the Endless Sky."

"That sounds to me like a lonely place to be ruler of."

"Just you and me. We can rule our lands together. We'll rule, unchallenged, until the end of time. We'll grow old together, just the two of us."

"Look at yourself!" said William, seeing their shared reflection in the silvery water. "You look old *already*, you fool!"

He wasn't wrong. Lingering in their watery domain, their skin had wrinkled like the faces of the elders.

"So . . . do . . . you . . ." said Kwame, parodying the creaky, frail speech of those elders. He walked hunched over, wobbling farcically over the smallest of stones, as if he were lame.

"Thank . . . you . . . loyal . . . subject," William mockingly struggled to say.

Back at home, they would have been beaten for this bare-faced irreverence; in the reclusive confinement of the cove, they knew there was hardly any danger of that.

More than an hour passed in which they frolicked in the water, accumulating scrapes and gashes from the barbed rocks that they wore boastfully as badges of courage. All through that hour, they swam hard, pushing themselves to the limit of their capacity and of their nerve. Yet each secretly had kept something in reserve, knowing that, once on shore, they'd run their traditional foot-race; a hard-fought dash along the boundaries of the inlet, in a show of speed and nerve that would test them both. They didn't just want to win the race, they wanted to push each other further, to run faster, to be the strongest men they could be. Strength, after all, was what they valued most, for it was strength – not eloquence, not learning, not a fair appearance – that defined a man as being successful. And each in his own way dreamed of being successful.

The contest was to begin on the first sound of the

warbler's song, but it wasn't a song they could agree on, so several false starts were recorded. Soon enough, the chase was on in earnest. They ran up the crumbly dunes, each losing valuable momentum as the sands cratered under the weight of their dusty feet. They careered around and sometimes under the brushwood, collecting more scratches from the cream-colored flowers and bristly spikes of the mangrove shrubs. William, enjoying a comfortable lead, had time to catch his breath, to regain his force for the grueling last leg of the course, and to undermine Kwame's confidence by gleefully deriding his friend's performance.

It was no surprise that William should win the race. He invariably did. Given his commanding physique and his prodigious height, the outcome was never in question. He was as agile as any of the other men. A build of swollen muscle, his shoulders were broad, his hands large and steady. His clothes seemed always too slight for his imposing carriage, his walk always as straight as the barrel of a rifle. Nevertheless, at first sight – with high-arched cheek bones and oval eyes of flint separated by a prominent nose – his face could appear almost rotund. It was quite the counter to Kwame, whose lean, sinewy, still immature features might have been mistaken for frailty, though he was as much a paragon of fitness as his friend. Still, William's staunch bearing was unerringly captivating, and the physical space he occupied so formidable, that visitors couldn't fail to notice him. They would fix on the wide mouth and lush lips his mother had handed down to him, half-expecting him at any moment to speak, and likely to say something prophetic. In truth, he was slow to do so. When eventually, warily, he did speak, his delivery was as strong and as resonant as an echo down a canyon wall. Across his face there reigned a dignified air, with a refinement and a concentration so noble, it seemed inevitable he should one day command an army of men.

William's superiority was not accidental, it was intentional, calculated even. It derived from a binding consciousness of his preeminent rank, and of the advantages that such a rank endowed. Those around him, too, were well aware of his primacy, and especially of his arresting physical attributes, and none more so than Kwame, who had come to rest his perspiring head on William's welcoming shoulder. Still, over time his younger friend had been catching up with William, gaining in strength and in confidence. He was becoming more of a threat in their foot-races as well, and they both knew it.

"One of these days, I'm going to win," said Kwame. "You know that, don't you? That must make you nervous, no? And just a little sad."

"I'd only be sad if I actually thought it were true."

Kwame, convinced of his looming victory, was resolute in his provocation. "Of course it's true. You're just blind, that's all. I nearly passed you on the last hill this time."

"Did you, really? I hadn't noticed. Listen, my friend, if you ever *do* out-run me, and let's just assume it's not because you started well before me or because I've snapped my leg in two pieces, I'll be the first to congratulate you. No, I'll bring out the whole *village* and insist they make an offering to you. We'll carve a statue of your tiny head. We'll make more of a fuss over you than they're making today over my dolt of a brother."

"Yeah, he *is* a bit of a show-off, isn't he?"

"That's for sure. So he went to France, and he came back. That doesn't seem much like heroism to me, I don't care how much adventure *you* think is out there."

"But don't you think he saw danger, William?"

"No, I don't think so. I don't think so at all. He's never been particularly courageous, my brother. He's happier to stay at home with the girls than to go hunt with the men in the forest. So I don't imagine he did much combat in their big cities. Besides, he's gotten so fat! Did you *see* him? He wouldn't have had much time for sword fighting or whatever tests they put foreigners through, when he must have just sat around all day eating their rich food."

"Are there many foreigners in France? Do you think there were lots of other people like Badu there?"

"No, not really. Despite what the teacher likes to tell us, that we're all the same to their god . . . Well, Father tells me, that's a lie. A *big* lie, and they don't even let people from their own colonies come to their country."

"Why not?" asked Kwame, much more disposed to believe his faithful friend than he did any dubious teacher.

"Well, why do you *think*? They don't want us to mix with their wives!"

The thought of that alone, of mingling with white women, or with any women for that matter, was enough to plague Kwame's imagination. He knew even less about the mystery that was womankind than he did about the distant, obscure land of France. The girls at home, his sisters, were impenetrable riddles to him, their behavior erratic, their moods terrifying. He might rather have faced a succession of swordfights, such as the ones he assumed Badu had endured, than negotiate a single hour on his own in the company of a woman. At least he understood the perils involved in swordplay; encounters with women seemed far riskier than that.

"You'd better be careful, William, before one of these days they ship *you* off to Europe."

"Just let them try. I'll run away if they do."

"I'll go with you," replied Kwame, abidingly devout.

"Ha. You couldn't keep up with me," joked William. "Not even if I gave you that head start."

They continued to needle each other with this easy banter until the daylight dwindled around them, but by then William's focus was redirected. He was already beginning to consider, and to fear, what it really would mean to be next to go.

His icy fear was closer to the truth than he could have imagined, for not a month later Chief Kurentsi was bound-up in conference with the governor, where the terms of William's prospective journey to England were being debated. Even as the joyous celebrations for his brother's homecoming began to collapse into blurred memory – the wreaths of flowers discarded and the thatched roof leaking once again – plans were being laid for the chief's second son to board another of the visitors' ships. To accept the false ingratiation of groveling hosts, and then to return with both his father's coffers and his father's influence amply fortified. Before another year was out, he would be ordered to undertake an expedition into the remote, veiled wilderness of Europe, sacrificed to his father's ambitions just as indifferently as his brother had been before him.

## • CHAPTER 4 •

The great limestone staircase had once been a marvel. Its compact stone had been borne of stratified sand and mud, and of the skeletal remains of immeasurable hapless creatures ensnared in the wake of a furious, ancient cold-spring river. A thousand million years later, those colorless carcasses, drowned or crushed by the merciless waters, would find new life, in a kind of defiant redemption. They bound together to form glassy white rock and lustrous, grainy crystals. The murderous river itself had long since been forgotten.

More than a century before, English builders ordered this raw stone to be cut into broad slabs and blocks as uniform as cadets in a Roman infantry regiment, and set against each other in just as perfect a formation. Collectively they formed an imposing flight of steps leading down to the huge vaulted rooms of the old fort. These soaring rooms were built to stockpile the vast supply of goods brought from Europe to Annamaboe, and the seemingly inexhaustible quantities of local gold for which these imported riches were traded.

But the supply of that gold had begun to falter. As it did, the majesty of the stairs began to ebb as well. The pristine stone had been corroded by salt deposits from the sea. It was battered by years of traffic and by the massive weight of goods being hauled in and out. At the top of the stairs, distressed rocks and knotted weeds now encumbered the once grand access. That entryway had since been condemned, replaced with a new, wider opening on the land side of the crumbling structure, shielding it from the more cruel ravages of the wind and the sea.

Today there was little suggestion left of that erstwhile rich trade, apart from the reddish pulp of palm fruit and cracked shells embedded in the stone. A few bits of string, and illegible notes that once held a record of the rooms' contents, had survived. Like the shells, fragments of that notepaper had gradually become wedged into fractures within the limestone, though they were hardly recognizable as paper any longer. The walls had been emptied of their shelving, dispossessed of the urns and clay pots and copper caskets that once occupied this yawning, underground hole. A hole that had long ago been converted into a vast dungeon for slaves. Like the captives thrown into these cells by the hundreds, the vaults had been stripped bare. All that remained on the sodden walls were rusted chains, and remnants of the fingernails and blood of those who had tried to claw their way to freedom.

In vain. For it was here, in this lurid pit, that freedom was truly extinguished. It was here that faith and confidence and promise methodically surrendered. Not a single prisoner had ever escaped this place; the iron bars that enclosed them were too strong, and the shackles that constrained them, too tight.

Not even the scant air was spared this terrible sanction. While the wind above roared, below ground there was no ventilation. Any fresh air that might briefly have lingered at the entrance, especially when the large mahogany doors were opened to let in a new wave of prisoners, made a hasty retreat, since only evil and darkness could live in these rooms. The few patches of light that did manage to seep through gaps in the cross-barrel brick ceiling were soon snuffed out, leaving only a ghostly obscurity, and the trenchant smells of urine, excrement and decay.

The heavy wooden doors penned in not only the prisoners, but any cries that tried to slip away as well. Cries from those who, from panic or from instinct, still thought it advantageous to let out their futile pleas for salvation. Their hoarse pleas were drowned out by those brisk winds above, by the crashing tide below, and by the careful distance between this subterranean prison and the massive construction of the new fort rapidly taking shape. Even if some faint sound were able to make its way across that broad divide, it would have been treated with disinterest by any of the builders or soldiers within its range.

This morning the wailing laments were particularly shrill, as a newly arrived contingent of captives was separated by sex, only then to be packed so tightly against each other that they could barely move. How fearful it was for each of them to realize that this accursed ordeal was not simply a long night's bad dream.

Any thought it might be just a dream or a fading hallucination was shattered by the unmistakable sound of rats chewing at the corpses of those who had perished from starvation, or those who had perished from fear. For many, that death would soon be welcomed, allowing their confounded souls to flee from the numbed bodies that entrapped them before they could be conquered. It would be a relief not to endure the unrelenting suffering they knew, or they well assumed, was still to come.

In an appalling paradox, the death of a slave in this

iniquitous keep could be a useful outcome for his master as well, since it tended to increase, if not the volume of his cargo, then at least its value. It was an efficient way to weed out the weak, whose spent bodies were thrown over the fort's retaining wall and into the sea, while the stronger ones would, in a month or two, be marched awkwardly onto waiting ships. What's more, those who took that ominous march, who survived for weeks in the wretched conditions of the fort's dungeon, had their spirit solidly broken even before their conveyance arrived. This only ensured they'd prove more docile passengers on the long, difficult journey to the Americas.

\* \*

It was to the new fort, towering high on the natural ramparts of the coastline, that Chief Eno Kurentsi and a retinue of his subjects were making their way.

"Come on men, make more noise," said the chief. "Bang your weapons, beat your drums. Louder. Faster. I want to be sure they can hear us coming."

"I don't think we can make ourselves any louder than this, Father," said Badu, acting today not only as oldest son, but as deputy as well. "If we beat the *djembe* any harder, the skin might break."

"Well, tell them to shout then. I want everyone to stop and take notice. We should arrive like . . . like thunder."

"Why? Why does it matter? Look how many men we have. There must be forty or fifty of us. The governor's got to be impressed just by our numbers."

"Listen son, why do you think they're putting up this new building, right there where it'll dominate the seafront? For the view?"

"Maybe," said Badu, full of hesitation.

"No. They're doing it because they think it'll intimidate me. That it'll bully me, or be some kind of warning. Well they're wrong. If anyone's going to do any bullying around here, it'll be me. I'm not afraid of anyone, however big their fort or however many cannons they aim at me."

"So we shout at them, Father?"

"Yes. Tell our men to roar. To roar like the lions they are in their hearts. And just like the lion, we'll taunt our prey before we get close enough to bite."

And so the men whooped and howled as loudly as they could, making their way slowly enough up the hillside to the encampment so that all those watching, and not least the waiting governor, could properly take the measure of the chief and of his power.

"Don't the English already know we're coming, Father?"

"Of course they do. I sent a messenger, informing them the priests had chosen this day for my visit, and telling them to prepare for my arrival."

"They did? The priests agreed on a date? They never agree on anything!"

"Those fools, they wouldn't dare have kept me waiting. They knew how eager I was to make this trip, to see the state of this new camp for myself."

"Well they chose well in any case. The heavens seem to support them. There's not a single cloud in the sky."

"Even the heavens, son, follow my command. And those rotten English, they'll do as I say, too."

But the chief's confidence in his own authority was profoundly misplaced. The garrison troops, seasoned veterans to a man, looked blithely on the approaching column of men and boys with a mixture of disdain and studied insult.

They were quite accustomed to this kind of feckless charade. They had seen it all before, and weren't at any risk of being rattled by what they saw as such risible attempts at intimidation.

Even within his own forces, the further back in the advancing ranks one went, the more the chief's rigid discipline fell away. The stragglers at the rear positions were too easily prone to distraction – by the lively ribbing of the other men, by the punishing heat that sapped their already diminished force, by the stream of pretty girls on the roadside who had come out to behold the colorful and clamorous advance.

No one was more distracted than William and Kwame, who banged their drums and bandied their painted spears as instructed, but without interest. Until, that is, they got closer to their destination, and the scale of the works underway at the feverish site began to come into sharper focus. It stopped them both short.

"Would you look at that," said Kwame. "This place is going to be *enormous*. I bet you could fit two of the old forts inside it. Maybe three. And I bet you'll be able to see way out to sea from the top. Aren't you curious, William?"

"Sure I am. Of course I am," he replied. "I just don't know why we have to make such a fuss about it, marching here with such formality, like the priests filing into the temple. Why do we need all this show? All this trouble? What a waste of time and effort. It means nothing. Nothing at all."

"Well, *I* think it's impressive."

"What is? This little march of ours? We're just showing off. And just wait, it won't be long until they do the same thing. Exactly the same. We try to scare them, slapping our drums and with our pikes drawn. They'll try to scare us, too. Mark my words, soon enough they'll start showing off their guns, pointing their rifles at the sun so the brass shines right at us, like mirrors. Or they'll start beating their own buckets and pots, or whatever they've got up there, right back at us. But not like it's some kind of parade, to greet us. No, it's not to honor us Kwame, but to alarm us. Not to show us respect either. No, we don't respect each other, that's for sure."

"I respect them."

"No you don't. You fear them. That's not the same thing. We fear each other. And which side's better off for it? Not us, I can tell you that. Not our tribe, who might just as easily end up like our cousins in the north, who come to this place in chains. And not the white man either. Those poor souls, so far from their own villages, guarding a fort that one day we're bound to take from them. Or that one day will simply crumble into the sea, like the old one is."

"So why do we do it, William? Why do we even bother?"

"Well, I can tell you why Father does it, at least. He's organized this elaborate visit today as a demonstration of force. He's worried that if we don't show signs of strength every once in a while, we might lose our advantage and our privileges. That somebody else might take our place."

"Who?"

"Another tribe, maybe. Another chief. And maybe he's right. And I'm *sure* he's right to want to protect what he has. What *we* have. Their gifts and their money means he can buy all that cattle. To drink and smoke as much tobacco as he likes. He can cover my mother and the other women in decorative beads and shiny jewels and the cloth from Europe the women like so much. But, really, does my father's wealth make us a better tribe? Does it make *him* a finer man?"

"He's certainly powerful," said Kwame.

"Powerful, yes. But is he a better man because of it? He's important, and yes he's powerful, because we fear him, like we fear these soldiers and their modern weapons. Everyone does. And that's precisely the same thing that motivates the Englishmen. It's what makes them feel . . . It's why they feel necessary. Useful. It's why they get medals from their king, for their courage and daring against the likes of us. But they're not important. None of us is. Who will remember these men, Kwame, in fifty years? In a hundred years? Who will remember *us*?"

William hadn't expected an answer to his question, and none was forthcoming, for by this time Badu stood over the pair, wearing an ugly scowl on his face like an angry poison.

"Father said to make more noise," he said. "Didn't you hear him? Shout. And bang your *djembe*, or I'll bang your heads!"

So they obliged. Although in a gesture of private rebellion, William began to pound his own drum with almost cartoonish enthusiasm. He struck the instrument in a series of exaggerated, flailing swipes, like a fledgling heron spryly flapping his wings but who can't quite manage flight. And as his older brother walked away to rejoin the head of the column, William grunted an expression the English tutor had unwittingly taught him and that lately had become his favorite. "Sod off," he couldn't help but hiss. His young friend, as usual, couldn't help but laugh.

\* \*

The new governor, Thomas Marsh, heard the drumbeats. He listened from the room the men had named "the Hutch," an austere chamber in the old fort kept for his personal use at the top of the crippled staircase, not thirty feet from the squalid slave quarters below. From here, he could clearly make out the throaty shouts of the chief's approaching battalion. He wasn't a bit daunted. Like the battle-scarred forces under his command, he wasn't likely to be moved by this false swagger. His only concern was the pretense that would be required for the chief's inaugural visit; a pretense of friendship and deference as hollow as the rotted trunk of the long dead sycamore still crowding the bustling quadrangle.

Not that he wasn't minded to be amicable on meeting the Fante chief for the first time, for the governor strove always to embody the Church's benevolent teachings. He didn't wear his piety like a straight-jacket; it didn't sentence him to starched dogmatism or bigotry. Rather, his theology had preached tolerance above all. It was the strict exercise of that tolerance toward all the men he had led, regardless of their confession or communion, that had earned him their almost universal admiration – whether in Silesia, in Bavaria, or in this bleak posting, in the furthest remove from his native Gloucestershire he could ever have allowed himself to imagine. Yet it was an injunction, he knew, that would be strongly challenged in such an idolatrous land as this, in which his counterparts were as likely to be contemptuous of the Christian God's love as they were to be ignorant of it.

Not least, Governor Marsh had decided early to make the best of this microscopic outpost of the Empire to which he and his unflappably loyal and strikingly beautiful wife Abigail had recently been consigned. Others might have seen it as exile; he chose to see it as a reward for his trusted service, an unequivocal vote of confidence in his loyalty, and one that a less intrepid man might have felt compelled to decline. Most of all, he chose to see in this posting a blessing from God. One that hereafter would ensure both the solidity of his position within the king's armies, and the assurance of prosperity for his family.

So he was inclined to be content with his new circumstances. And today, he was especially resolved to be attentive to, and cordial with, the chief. His instincts, however, were to keep a certain distance. These were also his instructions. He knew well that many of the incumbents before him had been routed by squandering their objectivity and by cozying up to the natives, effectively renouncing much of their already shaky leverage in negotiations over the terms of trade. These terms, time and again, proved less favorable than the Crown had expected, and ultimately less than it could abide.

Thomas Marsh would not repeat these mistakes, for he was too dutiful an agent of the imperial cause. One could be forgiven for thinking he had just been cut out from the chiseled busts and expressionless portraits that lined the halls of the military academy at Woolwich. Like these men, his sense of dedication to the mission was uncompromising. And like the dinosaur eggs and stuffed dodos displayed around London in curiosity collections, his open-eyed effigy would one day be held up as a shining example of a dying breed. "Here, ladies and gentlemen," the docents would say, pointing to his wax likeness, "was a model soldier. There aren't many of this ilk still around."

But even on this busy morning, though it appeared to most as if he were following military code and procedures to the letter, a number of small, almost frivolous details betrayed his less than scrupulous application of the army's more fatuous regulations. The sound from the bankrupt garden of a dog barking, incessant since sunrise and only aggravated by the approaching agitation below, was evidence enough of that. For the governor had smuggled abroad his wife's beloved Norfolk spaniel, whose freckled, heavy white coat and comically long, feathered ears had quickly made him a familiar fixture around the settlement. He'd done this despite the months' long quarantine rules that forbade not just the unchecked importation of animals to England, but more curiously, their exportation as well. Abigail would never have forgiven Thomas if her most adored companion had been left behind, so there was never really a question of consenting to the official restrictions.

All morning the governor had put up with the dog's irksome yapping. In an effort to muffle the disturbance, he reluctantly got up from the folding camp-bed on which he'd been lying, and closed the room's one, rickety sash window. Turning back, he stopped to adjust the simple crucifix above the bed that had tilted to one side. Strictly speaking, it, too, was a departure from formal rules. Not that he wasn't permitted to display the religious image; where he had deviated was to hang the cross slightly higher – only an inch or two – than he had hung the portrait of his king. Only he would have noted the breach, though it was quite deliberate. He did so as a discreet sign of obeisance to what he understood as the ultimate authority. After all, the motto was clear enough: "For God, King and Country." And in that order. It was that order, and that authority, he intended to honor by this modest act of bravado.

By now, however, the drumming of the chief's forces had become so marked, the pulse of the marchers so close, that it again shook the cross. He watched the object's gentle swing on the wall as if it were a subtle dance conducted for his sole benefit. He studied anew the understated object, the astral serenity on the face of Christ, even as he prepared to dress into his full summer uniform.

That process, of dressing in his flamboyant army livery, was a long and a fastidious one. Slowly, he put on the gleaming white silk stockings, careful not to tear them, then fastened up the short black, canvas splatter-dashes on his feet. He tightened the rigid shirt collar around his neck, though he knew it would prove disagreeable in the savage heat. By contrast, without enough starch on hand to stiffen the regimental lace, his shirt cuffs were left to droop gracelessly.

Most laborious of all were the double row of buttons, ten on each side, on the thin, red wool coat he wore. It was these studs, along with the yellow facings, that were the defining feature of the uniform. But it was a maddening challenge to keep them as polished as they were meant to be, even though they had already been cleaned for him yesterday by one of the lance corporals.

As he began to buff the buttons again, he whistled softly the tune of his most favored psalm, the one he and Abigail would sing loudly with their congregation on Sundays. It was a kind of constant affirmation of their faith, especially the first verse, which read:

> *From all that dwell below the skies,*
> *Let the Creator's praise arise;*
> *Let the Redeemer's name be sung,*
> *Through every land, by every tongue.*

Such divine poetry seemed to him especially germane in such an alien land.

Between the many buttons on his coat, not to mention the breeches and belt underneath it, it took Governor

Marsh a good quarter of an hour to finish dressing. Plenty of time to ruminate about his first meeting with the chief, and plenty of time, as well, to sing the holy psalm, over and over again.

Having done up all the buttons, and having straightened the tasseled epaulette on his right shoulder, he checked himself briefly in the glass. In doing so, he caught a glimpse of the slave girl sniveling in the corner on the floor, her clothes in tatters. The comely young girl he just moments ago had raped. Cowering like a wounded animal. Trembling like the frightened child she was.

# • CHAPTER 5 •

Shutting the door to the Hutch firmly behind him, Thomas Marsh stopped on the landing of the foundering building to brush away the stray leaves and fallen twigs, as if tidying up the wind-swept patio of his country home. He paused to inspect the rising gunnery wall opposite, close to completion, where spectacular new ordnance would be installed by week's end. He had, however, already worked out that the equipment being assembled would serve more as a deterrent than as practical weaponry since, like their outmoded predecessors, the modern guns were never likely to be supplied with enough fodder for them to be effective, or at least to be effective for long.

Glancing upward, he spotted the dim outline of his wife Abigail in the bay of one of the high, turreted windows. From this vantage point, the entire structure suddenly appeared to him curiously antiquated, erected as it might have been from long-yellowed plans that should have been surrendered to the plunder of time. If he squinted, he could see the new fort as a medieval castle: its sturdy architecture sweeping upward in a colorless square shell, the slits in those turrets on the eastern wall allowing in but the tiniest dollops of light. It was typical of a form that, to an engineer, would have seemed modern a century or two before, but here the form it was ultimately taking would be suitable only as a defensive position, not as a place of comfort. It would certainly not offer anything like the opulence one might have been fortunate enough to find in a princely castle nestled somewhere in the Arcadian provinces of England.

Abigail already understood this and was greatly troubled by it, from the almost total lack of amenities, to the barren walls through which a stinging draft circulated. Today, however, she had more pressing concerns. She felt a deep anxiety in the pit of her abdomen that only built with the increasing advance of the chief's escort. And though she managed a smile to her husband waving from far below, she felt not so much relief in his coming to her as a kind of paralytic fear that the day's loathsome events were ever closer at hand.

Thomas would try to mollify her. But any words the governor could contrive to do so would at best be improvised and unconvincing, for he too didn't quite know what to expect at this nearing appointment.

"Abigail, don't you look pretty," said the governor, as he entered her dressing room, nearly breathless from climbing the high stairs. "Do let me help you with your dress."

"Thank you, Thomas. It's such a fine dress, except for these ribbons! They're so fussy, I can't quite seem to manage them." Seeing his unusually worn features, she continued, "But you look quite done in, dear. Have you been hard at work?"

"Yes, of course. Paperwork. And so *much* of it. I don't think I could've guessed there'd be quite so much administration to take care of here. Anyway, don't you worry about that. Let's just be sure we're ready for the chief's arrival. We don't want to keep him waiting. Not today. This meeting's going to be unpleasant enough without our giving him any excuse to reproach us."

"Oh Thomas, honestly, why do you need me there? What can I possibly add to the conversation?"

"But this is where you shine, Abigail. It's where you're at your best. And you'll be such a succor to me. Why don't you try to imagine we're entertaining at home?"

"At home I'd have fretted over the menu, not over the guests."

"The chief is an honored guest, just the same."

"It's not the same though, dear, is it? I won't be at ease in his presence. I'm shuddering just thinking about it." As she spoke, she dropped one of the silver ribbon clasps she'd been holding in her right hand. An unlucky accident, as it would prove difficult to find such a slight object among the mutinous jumble on the floor around her.

In fact, the state of the whole upper floor, the large rooms reserved for the Marsh's personal quarters, was somewhere between pandemonium and anarchy. It was a maelstrom of clutter. Half-opened crates and partially covered furniture competed with upended piles of leather-bound books and wax candles and stacks of pressed linen, all of which spilled into the teeming rooms like ocean castaways on a sandy reef. The many souvenir ornaments and carefully framed pictures they had taken with them from England, crowded on the floor, attracted not compliments, only dust, awaiting a decision from their mistress as to their final resting place. A decision that was not anywhere in evidence, since every choice Abigail would have to make, to place an object here or to hang a picture there, meant conceding just a fraction more to staying in this ill-favored place. The inevitable result, however, was the very opposite of the kind of well-run military command to which her husband was accustomed.

He might have been reprimanded if an envoy of the Royal African Company had turned up for an inspection – something that was always threatened in principle, but that rarely happened in practice. These visits had trailed off long ago, under the burden of their considerable expense, and because so many of the inspectors had been thwarted by disease and by other scourges, but mostly because the service had simply stopped bothering.

"Abigail dear, please do calm down. You've got to find a way to compose yourself in front of these natives."

"No, I can't say that I *will* find a way."

"Well, an unfortunate thing that would be, too, since we're likely to be living here for quite some time. You didn't think we'd come to Annamaboe without having to interact with them, did you?"

"No, of course not. I just . . . I mean . . . Well, you won't let him in my home, will you? The chief, I mean."

"What would you have me do? What's the alternative? You may not have grasped this yet, dear, but in many ways, we are completely hostage to him. And not just for the supply of slaves, but for a workforce, too. We couldn't build this fort, this home of ours, without local laborers. And we're going to need them to provide our essentials."

"Won't we be supplied by the merchant ships from England?"

"Apart from their paid loads, the ships only really carry enough supplies to provision themselves, and some simple rations for the forts. Without these local men, we'd be adrift."

"Would we really?"

"Most definitely," continued the governor. "And frankly, it's the chief's people who are going to have to start doing the cleaning up around here as well. None too soon,

I'd say. Goodness knows, what a shock it would've been for some English housemaid, if we'd managed to convince her to come out all this way. I can't say I blame your precious Mary for not wanting to come this far. Not here, of all places."

"And what a pity that is," said Abigail.

"Is it? Honestly, that Mary, with that prattling way of hers, was trouble enough for me. She caused me all manner of suspicions, that girl did. She and that tedious husband, they were always plotting something. I could never put my finger on it, but I'll be damned . . ."

"Thomas!"

"I mean, I'm pretty well certain of it."

"Mary plotting? Nonsense. If you want to talk about *real* plots, and a harrowing one at that, you need only look at what happened to poor Lady Greenleaf, that heartbroken widow. Those slaves of hers, they tried to . . . oh, what's the word?"

"Mutiny?"

"Mutiny. Yes, that's it. Mutiny. They well nigh cut her boys' throats in the dead of night. It was in all the papers. I meant to send her a note before we left, to console her, the poor dear."

Abigail Marsh had never met the Lady in question. In fact, she had hardly ever met anyone of elevated rank, though she aspired to little else. She did, however, have a singular talent, of convincing herself with great certainty that the lesser circles in which she moved only just bordered the rarified ones of her pretensions, and that these worlds would one day inevitably intersect. No evidence to this effect was too peripheral or too mundane. Effortlessly, she embellished every occasional brush with anyone of high-society into a tale of great personal consequence.

She did this so often and so adroitly as to come to believe her own woeful exaggerations. Every sighting of an uppity aristocrat or a gussied-up gentleman was retold almost as if she had shared an intimate supper at their home. Waiting beside a peer for a carriage, or seated at church services next to a senior cleric in white vestment, was soon parlayed into an amusing anecdote, full of fabricated detail. None of her tales was more wildly inflated than the story she would happily tell of how her husband received his present commission direct from the hand of the king, in a ritzy meeting room at Kensington Palace that overlooked the formal gardens, right as the spectacular planting beds were coming into bloom. None of this was accurate or truthful. Thomas Marsh had received his orders in an insipid office in Africa House in Leadenhall Street, and not from the king, but from a second-rate minister-of-state who, when handing over the necessary papers, couldn't even be bothered to rise from his scrappy leather chair.

Abigail had read about the alleged Greenleaf incident in *The Daily Courant*, and like many idle women of her class, was inclined to believe such flagrant propaganda. After all, such stories, more often than not apocryphal, served the interest of reader and editor alike, confirming as they did the view that slaves were at any moment capable of such violence. Not least, these stories helped to sell newspapers by the thousands, feeding the imagination and the fears of people as incredulous as the governor's wife.

"What poppycock," said the governor. "You and your ludicrous tales. You really ought to stop reading the rubbish in those papers, dear. Rest assured, the chief and his men aren't going to rise up, to mutiny. They're not going to challenge us. For starters, they've got too good a thing going here. Nobody gets richer than the chief does by our trade."

"They get rich, maybe, but at what price? They can only do so, Thomas, they can only keep this 'good thing going,' as you call it, with such brutality! The violence they're inflicting on their own kind . . . it's appalling. It's wicked. They drag these poor souls to your dismal cells, they chain up these men and women who seem quite indistinguishable from themselves. What's to stop them one day from turning on their own tribesmen for a little extra money, or from turning on us for that matter?"

"Abi, the Fante have a choice, and *this* chief in particular really understands this: they can either enslave others for profit – and a handsome profit at that – or they can be enslaved. It seems to me, their choice is an easy one. If I were in the chief's position, I'd do exactly the same. I even admire how he's managed it."

"Perhaps, but that still doesn't explain it. It doesn't justify why he must come *here*. Why must he come to my home?"

"He's coming to size up the new encampment. To size me up, too, I presume. And he's coming to seal the deal we talked about."

"Deal? What deal is that?"

"We've discussed it at length, Abigail. You remember, we're to send his son to London. His second son. These were my very first orders from the service. We're going to train him in our English ways."

"Train him in what? What has such a boy to learn from us that he could *possibly* use in this lost place?"

"We can teach him lots of things, dear, about business, industry, modern manufacturing, and capital. That's why the chief wants to see his William – that's his son, William – that's why the chief wants to see him go to London. So he can be educated. Properly."

"And presumably it won't hurt that it will only cement your relations with the chief himself?"

"Well yes, of course."

"But didn't you say his eldest son was sent to Paris? What can this boy learn in England that he couldn't learn in France?"

"Oh Abigail, you know well, the French have nothing to teach him. They are hedonists. Libertines all of them."

"Libertines?"

"They only care about luxury. They only know frivolity. They are not men of the world, men of business, like the English."

"Perhaps he might also learn something of our religion?"

This was a fanciful notion. The scattering of Anglican missionaries who, in the decades preceding had reached this far, had met with considerable resistance. They left a trail of prejudice and superstition that was not well tolerated among the Fante people, and that stained the faith. Some had been well-meaning, but most had been completely discredited, wreaking havoc and an ugly chauvinism, and were lucky to leave with their lives.

"Perhaps he will," said the governor, humoring his wife, though he knew this to be unthinkable. "So pull yourself together. Besides, it will all be over soon enough."

And precisely as the governor anticipated, the interview that soon followed took very little time indeed. It was a perfunctory affair, in which traditional gifts and niceties were exchanged with the proper show of decorum, but with nothing more. Elaborate, protracted negotiations proved unnecessary; the chief had long since made up his mind to send William to England. His interest, as always, was simply to extract the most profitable conditions he could manage. When it came to such matters, especially any re-lated directly to his own family, he would hold out for even more favorable terms than those he had secured for the pro-vision of slaves. This was something for which no one could fault him, since the chief's supply of sons was considerably more limited than that of the captives he could so reliably produce.

The only substantive item left to arbitrate was that of timing, but here too the chief would prevail, insisting that William's tour abroad would wait not for just any transport, but for a ship befitting a prince. He would await the next landing of the *HMS Lady Carolina*. She was the most splen-did, and so for the chief, the most fitting of English ves-sels to make the journey from Annamaboe to London and back again, by way of distant Barbados, a land about which the chief knew very little, except that it continued to en-rich him. His son, it was agreed, would gain passage when the famous ship next made port, in just over a year's time. Time enough for William to brace himself for a mission he had never sought, and to try to earn his father's still ambiva-lent respect, which he sought always.

"The chief's not going to have his way with you when he enters our home," said the governor, "if that's what you're concerned about."

"Thomas! What an absolutely dreadful thing to say," replied Abigail, stopping to compose herself again. "You know, Lady Greenleaf was glad to get rid of the Africans in *her* home, I can tell you. I should be glad of it, too."

"Well, I'm glad to be rid of your Mary. Put that in your newspaper."

"Oh Thomas, you're impossible," she said.

Livid at her husband's churlish and unkind talk, Abigail reciprocated in the only way she could think of, by making them late for their imminent meeting with the chief. She would drag out her dressing just long enough to exasperate him. And so, turning back to her mirror, she discreetly untied a few of the ribbons Thomas had already so painstakingly helped her secure.

## CHAPTER 6

For very nearly a week, a shallow and listless constellation of frothy clouds could be seen loitering in the neighboring valleys, the closest not more than a few short miles away. And then abruptly, and without so much as a lone flash of lightning for warning, these solitary clouds conspired to form a single, burly mass, and began to shower their deliverance onto a grateful people below.

Here in Annamaboe, however, the gods had not yet been satisfied, and persisted in their fearful privation. Here, the people did not rejoice. Though they could hear the distant rumble of thunder, though they could see the gloomy fog on the near horizon, still the rains did not come. And if there was not yet a sense of alarm, there was a mounting sense of unease. Everywhere a pall of melancholy, almost despair, held dominion, accentuated by the shroud of scratchy dust that blanketed the land. Cinders of the scorched earth mingled with baked sand, blown inland from the seafront. It fused with flecks of powder-down from thousands of hatchling birds, and with the billowing seeds of the dried-out Baobabs, liberated from the jealous confinement of their normally tenacious leaves. Even the sugary pulp of the locust-beans worked itself free, dripping from extravagant heights to scar the already faded patches of grass around their roots, turning the ground a bittersweet shade of yellowed rust.

For days the priests had called for mercy. They led the pilgrimage to the sacred grove; they performed the customary rites and made the prescribed sacrifices. The women gathered to dance, synchronously and in tight circles, having fastened scores of feathers to their waists, in a challenge certain to entice the winds. The children looked on at this dance with a mixture of amusement and awe, the youngest among them troubled to see their mothers in a sort of trance, overtaken by the rapture of such well-rehearsed movements. The throbbing movements they made appeared to the children, for the moment at least, to be doing little other than exacerbating the very problem they were meant to solve, fomenting even more of the noxious grit that filled the stale atmosphere.

In the afternoon, however, the atmosphere and the mood began to change. Everywhere the light quickly dimmed and the colors of the landscape sharpened, before fading into obscurity. The air thickened with an aching heaviness, and with expectation. And then, at last, the reprieve came. It began as so often it did, with a rising westerly wind and then a sprinkling of velvety drops of crystal rain, soaked up ravenously by a worn-out land. Like sentinels, each blade of grass, every droughty leaf and fruit, seemed to stand at attention, impatient to receive its gift and to show its gratitude.

Ordinarily, the generous downpour and the fierce gusts that accompanied it would build and build in intensity. They would reach an electrifying climax, before the sky cleared its throat and ordered the soupy clouds to beat a retreat as quickly as they had come. But tonight, the power of the storm merely continued to strengthen. The rain crashed down with a delirious violence. Everyone waited patiently for the crackling thunder or for other suggestive signs that the violence would abate, but these signs of exhaustion didn't come.

Instead, the deluge sustained its wanton blows. It quickly snuffed out the remaining bonfires in and around the chief's compound. The arabesque motifs on the exterior walls of the main house – their precise geometry freshly painted in white pigments drawn from roots and berries and bark – had not yet had time to dry or to be covered in beeswax, so were washed away as handily as a chalk alphabet on a schoolroom blackboard. But these outcomes were predictable, and they were reparable; the sudden, wrathful onslaught also caused fallout that was far more damaging, and would prove far more laborious to put right. Every tight sheaf of wheat, standing solitary in a just harvested field, disintegrated into a tufted heap. Every well-travelled footpath was swallowed up by the bounteous syrupy mud that cascaded down the hillsides like an unhinged avalanche, drowning the soil it was meant to enrich. Worst of all, the straw roofs of out-buildings collapsed under the terrible weight of the streaming water, including the cramped shed that housed the compound's firewood, rendering that wood useless for days after.

Yet no one would see this damage until morning, when at last the assault waned. Until then, its startling savagery kept everyone indoors, and its unbroken roar masked all other sounds. Not least, the constancy of the rain, and the tremendous relief that it had finally come, eventually lulled everyone into a profound, contented sleep.

Everyone, that is, except William. For him, the peal of the downpour provided excellent camouflage, something he badly needed in order to cloak his skulking movements.

It disguised his tiptoeing across the drenched courtyard. It disguised, too, the lusty groan of the kitchen's wooden door he had just opened, one of the few in the house hung on wrought iron, barrel hinges provided by the English, though they hadn't thought to provide the oil to keep the fittings lubricated. What he hadn't counted on, however, was the near total darkness, so that even wearing his sandals he lost his footing on the dim, slippery steps, only narrowly avoiding falling headfirst onto the hard floor.

He knew he had only a few minutes, for beyond that he might all too well be discovered. He couldn't possibly have explained what he was doing there. He couldn't possibly reveal that he was pilfering whatever food he could find for an illicit tryst, a secret assignation the following day with a beguiling young girl called Esi.

\* \*

For many months, the pair had been meeting surreptitiously, without the knowledge of their families, and certainly without their approval. To keep these meetings secret was a minor triumph, a feat that had eluded so many others in a place where even trivial news – from the unexplained death of a single head of cattle, to a hunter's trifling injury – flew faster than a rifle shot. They managed to see each other twice a week, on market days when William would return with his older sisters from bartering the family's wares. They had chosen a sequestered spot not far from where he had first seen her several years before, as he passed through her village on his way to the bazaar. Back then, when both were still practically children, he had thrown her nothing but caustic glances; she threw nothing back but sticks. But neither of them was a child any longer. Just as soon as he was old enough, and when it was deemed to be safe enough, he travelled by himself to the market, lingering for lengthy periods in her village. Soon sticks were no longer being thrown, and any childish barbs between them had been recast as coy flirtations. Not long after that, these had ripened into furtive rendezvous, and these in turn had quickly ripened into love.

"You've done it?" exclaimed Esi. "You've actually gone and done it? Well, William, you surprise me once again. I never thought you'd pull it off."

"Pull what off?" he replied, pretending not to know what she meant, teasing out of her the requisite praise he knew would be forthcoming.

"This. This feast!" she said, pointing to the slapdash spread he'd laid out for her consideration. "When I challenged you, when I *dared* you to prepare a meal for me, for us, I never thought . . . well, I never thought you'd actually sneak into the storeroom of your father's house."

"Why wouldn't I? Don't you think I'm clever enough? Didn't you think I'd be brave enough?"

"Clever enough, yes," she replied. "But brave enough to defy your father's wives? I'm sure the women must keep track of where everything is, right down to the very last fig. No, I didn't think you were *that* crazy!"

"Oh, I don't worry about them. Well, most of them anyway. It's just my mother, Eukobah, she's the one who'd be most annoyed. She'd be unforgiving. She'd have beaten me about the head if she'd caught me."

"Beaten you how? Like this?" asked Esi, as she landed a lighthearted slap across the crown of his head.

On cue, William simulated an egregious injury. He pleaded both for leniency and for comfort. A comfort that could uniquely be afforded by the soothing kindness of her gentle embrace.

The soft remedy of Esi's touch, the charity of her kiss, had at first startled William, those many months ago. From afar, she appeared to him to shelter under a hard if beautiful shell. But he had mistaken her determination for hardness. It was that determination, that shrewdness, and above all a fearless will to succeed on terms she could herself designate, that most defined her. Such fearlessness could intimidate others, but it mesmerized William. This confident pluck, coupled with her private affections, was the very thing that had taught him – allowed him – to discard his haughtiness, and to leave any trace of arrogance or affectation behind. It allowed him, too, to discover and to celebrate the joys of love.

"This meal's a very small thing," he said. "There's *nothing* I wouldn't do for you. Only for you."

"Really? Only for me? I might have my doubts, if I listened to the gossip."

"What gossip?"

"Just some of the other girls talking, that's all," said Esi. "I hear them say you have a girl in *lots* of the villages," she added, not demonstrating enough confidence in her protest to convince even herself of this harmless fiction.

"Oh do they really?" he replied, professing mild offense.

"Yes, that's what they say. So . . . do you?"

"Do I what?" asked William, with total nonchalance.

"Have girls in other villages?!" she said, rankled that her ruse was not succeeding in inciting the vexed reaction she'd counted on.

"Esi, that's just the stupid talk of simple-minded little girls. You know full well, I can see no one but you," he replied, flitting the high arches of his eyelids like a hurried butterfly flaps its wings.

"So why then are those pretty brown eyes of yours looking at me like that?" she asked.

"Like what?"

"Like that. Staring squarely at me, with that odd grin frozen on your face. I don't know what to make of it exactly. It's like I'm . . . like I'm some kind of plaything that just amuses you. Do I amuse you, young man?"

"Charm me is more like it. Listen," he continued, taking her firmly in his arms, "*you're* what matters to me. The only thing, the *only* person I care for. That's how it is today, that's how it will be tomorrow. Forever. And the way I'm looking at you is exactly what it appears to be. It's simple really, I can't take my – what did you call them? – my pretty brown eyes off you. Not now. Not ever. Not even for a minute. Even when you're away, all these eyes can see is your face before me, like in a dream."

"What, *this* ugly face?" she asked, contorting her graceful features into a grotesque form, flattening her nose and crimping her mouth, like one of the brush-tailed porcupines they'd seen earlier.

"Yes, even *that* face. That beautiful face," said William, as he leaned forward and kissed her again.

It was a gesture to which she happily capitulated. "So I'm the *only* person that matters to you, is that it? Then what about your blessed sisters – how do I measure up to them?"

"My sisters? Oh don't you pay any attention to them. They are nothing to me. Really, nothing. They're not nearly as virtuous or as high-minded as they would have others believe."

"And what about your friend, Kwame, whose name never seems to be far from your lips? Whose company never seems far from your mind?"

"Kwame? That's funny! He's just an empty-headed, naïve little boy. He doesn't mean anything to me. He doesn't
matter. Not a bit."

"Is that so?"

"It is. If he left tomorrow, I don't think anyone would
even notice he'd gone!"

"So William – dependable William – you expect me to
believe this, that it's only *me* in your heart? That the sisters
who idolize you are nothing to you? That the boy who trails
you like a dog trails its master, who dotes on you – that
even him you don't hold dear?"

"I am telling you that, yes. I'm telling you, I would
trade a year of radiant days of sunshine with Kwame for a
single stormy day with you."

"And the girls in the other villages?"

"Esi, really, don't mind that laughable gossip. Don't be
suspicious. Let's not worry about *that* kind of thing. Let's
forget about everyone else for once and just . . . just admire
the sunset, which can't be long in coming."

"The sunset is still ages away. And we'll die from hunger first," she couldn't help but tease him. "I'm ravished,
aren't you? So, let's see what you've brought!"

"Alright then, here you go," said William, as he prepared the spoils.

His less than inspiring takings consisted of a mess of
barnacled oysters, half a loaf of bread, a jug of tepid water,
and an array of clay jars of various sizes and shapes.

"And what's this meant to be?" she asked, opening the
first jar.

"It's sugar. To sweeten the bread."

"Silly, this isn't sugar. It's flour. What are we to do with
flour?"

"Flour?" he said. "What do you mean?"

"It's millet flour, pure and simple. Were you hoping we'd have time to bake bread?" she mocked.

"I hope you're kidding," he said, examining a sprinkling of the powdered substance for himself, before it was quickly carried away on the strength of the still blustery winds, and he realized she wasn't.

Opening the second jar, Esi continued, "And ground kola nuts? What shall we do with these?"

"That's not kola, it's dried chili pepper. I've seen the women take it from this very jar plenty of times. It's to put on the oysters. Which, by the way, were a real worry to sneak out of the house quietly, I can tell you."

"What a shame then, since I'm afraid the oysters have gone bad. And this, this is most definitely *not* chili powder," she said, putting a pinch to her mouth to verify her assertion. "To start with, it's bitter, not spicy. Taste it," she continued, offering her finger to his lips in so voluptuous a manner, he couldn't possibly refuse.

"What a mess. You're right," said William, once he had time to recompose himself. "We're going to starve."

"Not at all. You underestimate me."

As usual, Esi had anticipated several contingencies, and had stashed provisions of her own in the cloth bag she invariably carried. In it there was plenty on which the couple could indulge: a crisp loaf of cassava bread, a pot of monkey-orange preserve, a handful of roasted egusi seeds, and enough scraps of bushmeat to more than ensure that neither of them would go hungry. As she prepared the food she'd brought, William looked away shyly, idly kicking the muddy gravel with his feet in a dispirited motion. He hovered uneasily, somewhere between embarrassment for the failure of his own planning, and admiration for the success of hers. Mostly, he was grateful, especially as they sat down to their simple meal, the kind no young lovers had ever enjoyed more.

The meal, however, was to be an abbreviated one, for hearing what Esi thought were voices nearby, she grabbed his hand and in one breath they tore deeper into the wood for cover. They needn't have concerned themselves. It wasn't any passerby they heard, just the excited jostling of animals, small and large alike, which had come to life in the aftermath of the storm. In fact, theirs was only one of many feasts to be savored that day, for the insects wrested from the safety of their hiding places, the worms unearthed from their sunken shelters, became a miraculous bounty for all manner of creature to enjoy. The birds, too, were circling overhead in their numbers, ready in turn to pick up their long overdue windfall.

Having found a dry spot on the banks of the river, still raging from the heavy rains, William and Esi laid down as one, reveling once again in the communion of each other's nakedness. This gift from the gods, this mysterious exaltation that, before they found each other, neither had known existed. For a while at least, time stopped. But only for a while.

"This has been the perfect day, William," she said, "but it's getting late. I've got to get dressed, and get back."

"It's not as late as all that."

"Yes, sadly, I'm afraid it is. Look, the sun's starting to go, and I can hear the bell in my village."

"That's not the bell in your village. It's the call of the English church."

"I wish you were right, William. I wish we could stay here for hours longer. But that isn't the English church, and you know that as well as I do. It's my village. And I'll be missed if I don't go soon. I've got to get home."

"You *are* home, Esi. Here with me," he said, in reaction to which she couldn't resist planting another passionate kiss on his eager mouth.

Leisurely, they walked back through the meadows, their hands cradled in a tender clasp. A firm grip that grew even tighter when they reached the open road, as they relished their last moments alone.

* *

But they were not alone. Kwame had trailed the progress of the amorous couple for most of the steamy day. He did so with growing disfavor, and with a growing distemper.

For Kwame, the younger of the two, William had always been the exemplar of incorruptible faith. His was the one devoted friendship that, through shared experiences and hushed confidences without number, had been tested again and again. They were as alike as two halves of a coconut, or two halves of their cherished canoe – sourced from the same tree, and inseparable. Theirs was an implicit exclusivity: they studied, played, dreamed together. Theirs was not so much a secret language, as one might observe among twin siblings, as subtle movements by which they communicated coded messages; they had spent so much time in each other's company, that through the flip of an eyebrow or the roll of an eye, each knew at once what the other was thinking. Despite the differences in their age and in their status, Kwame thought of them simply as each other's shadow.

Shadows, however, can be fickle. They can change with the weather, with the inclination of the shimmering sun, with time itself. And the length, the position of William's shadow was clearly changing. Not for the first time of late, Kwame felt he was losing its protection. He felt, bitterly and dolefully, that he was being betrayed.

And not just by anyone. He was being supplanted by a girl, no less, and girls were the enemy. This was an aberrant species, and the target of their almost constant derision. A curious breed that, it was long ago agreed, needed to be avoided at all costs. Girls were not allowed to know the boys' private code, to ride in their canoe, even to know about their retreat at Bogi Cove. And certainly they shouldn't be permitted to steal the attention and the intimacy of staunch friends.

At one point Kwame had gotten close enough to overhear their sentimental musings. He only wished that he hadn't, since what he heard offended him greatly. It incensed him. He'd heard William refer to him as emptyheaded. As naïve. To suggest in brutal and unambiguous terms that he, that their steadfast friendship, was of no consequence.

As he watched the young lovers separate at the roadside, Kwame sat by himself on a faraway hill, picking absentmindedly at the scab on his knee, the one he wore as a souvenir from the last foot-race with William. As he chipped away at the prickly scar, it began to break apart, trickling blood down his leg in a crooked pattern that mirrored his own meandering state of mind. He took no notice. All he could think about was his friend's treachery. All he could feel was that his faith and his trust had been broken. And by this time it wasn't only blood that flowed, but also tears that ran down his young face, burning his already inflamed cheeks. He just let them run.

By day's end, Kwame's grief had turned into anger. And his anger soon turned into outright indignation. He stewed on the injustice that had befallen him, all the way back home. It troubled him as he completed his round of evening chores. It would perturb his sleep as well, even more than the heavy showers which, after the hiatus of a sublime afternoon, were poised to return. Once again, the sky above was darkening.

# • CHAPTER 7 •

As if in procession, one by one the lone kingfishers lazily returned to their woodland habitat on the outermost edges of Annamaboe. The barn swallows, too, completed their epic migration, but in rhythmic swarms that gently heaved and swelled like ocean waves. Together, the returning legions of wearied birds could be forgiven for not recognizing the terrain as the withered one they had fled. For in their absence, the bruising rains had grudgingly retreated to an airy hibernation. But in that shy withdrawal, the seasonal floods bequeathed a forceful legacy of change, none more dramatic than the patchwork of spirited colors now covering the once pale landscape.

That pallor was nothing by then but an ambiguous memory. Everywhere, a sense of renewal governed. On the cursive hillsides, across the wide meadows and by the restless streams, in every direction the blue-green grasses had grown long and rooted, their narrow-leaf blades fluttering in the soft wind. Their luster provided a near-ubiquitous canvas upon which a riot of color was rollicking in bountiful triumph.

In a challenge to these pervading grasses and to the rolling fields of fragrant lavender, the giant hardwoods boldly and vainly proclaimed their own resurrection – and their own dominance – in ordering their plush red and pink flowers to bloom. They competed for favor with whole tracts of land erupting with radiant violet, pink and white orchids, their lately-wilted stems again standing tall. The hoary threads on their long, leathery leaves sparkled with restored life; like speckles on an egg, the promiscuous spots on their youthful flowers presented themselves proudly, their petals opening up seductively like inviting lips.

The harbor, too, hummed with new life. Ever since the seas had been pacified, the port was playing host once more to a staggering number of ships, from veterans who knew its shores well, to neophytes discovering the obliging waterfront for the first time. The ships were both military and commercial, both humble and grand, and all shared in the restful balm of her sanctuary.

Without question, the grandest of them all was the *Lady Carolina*. And after more than a year of travels to the New World and then back again to her home on the Thames, she had returned to the Gold Coast at last.

Once with some seventy guns to her name, this massive cutter was one of the first ships of the Atlantic fleet to boast three masts. Each one bore a unique medley of triangular headsails and bulky, square topsails. It was a combination that allowed for the harnessing of vast wind energy, and for unequaled speed. It was the craft's unusually long decks that had originally allowed for such a large cache of weapons to be carried into hostilities; since then, they allowed for more passengers and for more slaves to be carried than on any of her many rivals.

The hulking ship had been captured by the Royal Navy from the French two years earlier, in a hard-won, bloody battle in the Gibraltar Strait in which its luckless captain was drowned. After much quarreling in Parliament about the expense, it was agreed she was to be salvaged, converted for use in the merchant trade, and renamed. The much heralded conversion, however, proved cosmetic only, not least since so much of the funding allocated for the purpose was siphoned off as political patronage. So although on the surface she cut a splendid figure, her submerged frame was deeply corroded and decomposed. Swathes of timber in her hull lay infested with shipworm. From bow to stern the iron bolts that kept those planks in place lay rusted. With such complicated riggings, with multiple smaller jibs and a massive one that haughtily furled on her enormous bowsprit, the *Lady Carolina* required a highly trained and experienced crew to sail her. And those who sailed her, who knew their way expertly around her anatomy, knew she was grievously impaired.

The ship's seaworthiness was the subject of undying conversation, and of often rough debate, among her band of hardened men, just as it was this morning between three of the more garrulous – a collusive threesome that had formed over her recent journeys.

They were led by the ship's first mate. Assiduous in his responsibilities to protect her men and cargo, he was the most weathered seaman among them. The oldest hand on deck, he was called Spike, not because he had a character or a build as strong as a nail, but because of the long, thick, pointed scar on his jaw that resembled one. It was a souvenir of a brutal knife fight in La Coruña, in the lustiness of his youth, the object of which was long since forgotten to him, even if the physical expression of it was not. Crouched beside him on the quay sat Roley, the ship's cook, whose nickname was itself short for "roly-poly" and which required no knotty explanation. He was an unassuming man who had determined early never to let his lack of formal education hinder his congenial relationships with even the most senior and best-educated officers in the fleet. Nor for that matter did it impede his capacity to order the more junior men about, not least his assistant Clifton, or Cliff, the last of the gabby trio, who hadn't been sailing long enough to earn anything but the most straightforward of nicknames.

The three men, of contrasting background and ambition, all had an uncurbed appetite for three things: easy women, which presently were in short supply, and strong tobacco and even stronger liquor, of which there never seemed to be any shortage.

"You know about these things, Spike," said the cook. "And you've been with her longer than either of us. Longer than both us of combined, probably. Whadda ya give her? A year more? Two?"

"Oh, she's not that poorly," replied the first mate. "I've seen worse. Hell, so have you! A lot worse than this one. She'll manage to carry on for some time yet, alright. And she does still fly like the wind, I'll say that for her."

"Flyin' straight into hell, if you ask me."

"I'm with Roley," said the cook's assistant, Cliff. "My bet? We're all gonna end up treading water one of these days, stranded a couple hundred miles out there in the middle of the dark ocean, clinging to bits of wood and sail as she goes down like a stone." At the thought of his own grisly prophecy, of a speedy and pitiful drowning – which, for his sins, he knew no one at home would mourn – Cliff took a deep swill from the jug the men were sharing. It was a combustible concoction Roley had manufactured on board out of nothing but cornmeal, sugar and some old bread, all of which he tossed into a pressure cooker until it could be distilled into almost pure grain alcohol. It slipped down their greedy throats like honeyed fire.

"One more storm like the one we saw off Tangier," continued Cliff, "and this ship's a footnote in the history books, that's for damn sure."

"That wasn't a storm," said the cook. "That was a hiccup. A frog in the throat. Just you be patient, and you'll see a *real* storm soon enough. The kind of vicious gale that'll make you wish you'd never wanted to go to sea in the first place. It'll have you *prayin'* we was back in Tangier."

"Anyway, Cliff," said the first mate, "what do *you* know about the history books? You've never opened a book in your life."

"What of it? And even if that's true, I still know what they's gonna write about the *Lady Carolina*, 'cause she's got herself quite the reputation!"

"Damn right she does," replied the cook. "A noble reputation, and a hell of a history, which we's helpin' to write."

"What do *you* reckon they'll say about her, Roley, in those books?" asked Spike of the cook, as he stole a drag off his friend's pipe.

"Whatever they do write, I reckon they're gonna say, her end came swiftly, it came violently, and it came with glory. Just the way I want to go, come to think of it!"

Spike wasn't convinced. "I think they'll say," he retorted, "that like too many women, she started as a ravishing creature, but ended up a horrible wreck."

"Never known one that didn't," said the cook. "Not a single one that didn't sag and dry up over time."

"Me neither," confirmed Cliff.

"Never known one *what* that didn't sag, a woman or a ship?" asked the first mate.

"Both," the two others replied in unity, and set them all off laughing.

"Both, damn it," Roley just managed to squeak out again between spasms.

"Still, you have to love 'em, boys," said Spike. "Both of them – tough women, and a tough ship, like this old battle-axe. Lord knows I love my woman, waiting for me patiently as always, like an angel, back home. Just as I love this here relic of a ship."

"Nothing else but them matters," concurred Roley. "Just women and ships. Ships and women. Nothing else in this whole damn world's of any interest to me."

"I'll drink to that," said Spike enthusiastically, though he needed little such prodding to inhale more of the cook's venomous firewater.

By this time, they were all more than a little potted with drink. Unwisely so, since the long day ahead announced itself as a busy and taxing one. Each of them had his assigned role to play in the devilish choreography involved with the loading and unloading of the ship's payload. It was an intricate dance that required significant coordination, and precision timing, for there was no margin for error. The *Lady Carolina*'s schedule allowed it to be anchored for just two days in port; two short days that meant preparing to leave almost from the moment she landed.

The racing pace of that activity was only accelerating, and by late day most of the goods had been off-loaded. The ship had been relieved of several tons of supplies, soon to be dispatched not just locally, but to garrisons and command posts up and down the coast. The troops on duty at Annamaboe heartily received the takings of the fort – everything from ammunition for the light guns, to fresh uniforms for the men, to enough varieties of foodstuffs to cheer the governor's heartsick wife into believing she could at last prepare proper meals. She too was on hand, to inspect the jars of vinegar and pickles, the salted lima beans, the molasses and catsups she had requested, as well as the sumptuous spiced chocolates and tins of gingerbread she had not.

In a somber irony, many of the same exhausted captives who from tomorrow would sail away on the vessel, were required to help disgorge the very cargo that would make room for themselves. The rows and rows of stiff timber shelves, on which great quantities of merchandise were exported, were soon transformed into thorny plank beds by some of the same broken men and women who by morning would be tethered to them. They would be packed in even more tightly than the goods they were being charged to remove.

As they did so, the towering ship climbed higher and higher above the water line. Little by little, more of the Roman numerals of its draft marks, painted in white on the starboard side to gauge its depth, rose above the choppy water. Yet she didn't rise for long, since in exorbitant numbers those slaves were bundled and pressed, chained and manacled, into the lower decks.

The whole of this fevered enterprise had been planned and organized with implacable attention by the ship's young captain, a civilian by the name of David Bruce Crichton, for whom this command represented his first full commission, and this run only his second to West Africa. To many hardnosed observers, his appointment had been nothing short of astonishing – not only because of his youth and relative lack of experience, but because he had never exhibited any of the well-codified, consummate allegiances to the king, the kind of ostentatious expressions of loyalty that might have been expected of one seeking such a potentially lucrative post.

As a Scotsman, born in the same year as the Acts of Union were signed, he was raised like many of his northern countrymen to look on that treaty as treason. And though he might have concealed his resentments from the service well enough to secure his coveted commission, once at sea he hadn't tried to hide them from his mostly English sailors. Worse still, neither had he hid his aversion to the crew's long-established rituals and, in his estimation, their inane protocols. To them, however, he operated boorishly, without due courtesy, and more like a pirate than a senior commissioned officer might have done. Indeed, he wouldn't have found unflattering their comparison of him to a mercenary, for in truth he would happily have worked under the flag of any country if it were willing to pay him more.

In many respects, Captain Crichton was in the mold of the ship itself: a strong and imposing appearance, but rotten at his core. Talking to him was like conversing with the tall suspicion of a ghost; so cold and distant was his stare, it seemed a kind of pathology. He wore a perpetually twisted expression that could have been mistaken for a deformity. It was not a defect, or the function of some brutal physical pain, but rather the severe, persistent fury of a villain. His rancorous stare was made more prominent still by the way his jet-black hair had been slicked back over his temples. The veins in those temples and on his lanky neck flared up as easily as did his temper. He used his low, baleful voice and torturously slow Scottish drawl to pour scorn and ridicule on his men.

The captain had issued the strictest of instructions that, without fail, everything was to be unloaded from the *Lady Carolina* by nightfall. Everything, that is, except for a sizable consignment left untouched in one corner of the main hold. The claim on this shipment was held by Chief

Kurentsi, and contained a mixture of his favorite goods ordered specially and, as always, a collection of trappings from the English government meant as tribute for his enduring cooperation, all of which Captain Crichton ordered to be left unmoved. Even now, he and the governor were arguing about this decision in the courtyard of the fort, with a bevy of soldiers and a handful of the ship's party looking on with only the faintest of interest.

"That chief of yours, Marsh, he owes me ten guineas for the *last* shipment. He's a fool if he thinks he's getting his hands on *this* lot before he owns up for the *last* one."

"The chief owes you nothing," shot back the governor. "I won't hear of it."

"You won't *hear* of it? Won't *hear* that the cad stiffed me? Well whether you want to listen to it or not, I'm telling you, I won't give him a thing from that load 'til he pays me that debt of his. Every penny of it. He owes me that gold for the last shipment, and it's just not proper he should get a single bit of anything new, anything I took the trouble to drag all the way here, before he makes good."

"You ass, Crichton. This is not yours to decide. There are bigger interests at stake here. Much bigger, and forces you couldn't possibly understand. Political forces. Considerations of Empire."

"I couldn't care less about any *forces*. Any Empire. There's only one thing I care about, and that's my purse."

"Well, that's hardly surprising, young man," retorted the governor.

"Are you aiming to insult me, is that it? Scare me? Listen here – what those chaps in the Royal Company, or whatever they're called these days, what they cook up back home doesn't have anything to do with me. Not a whit. Me, I've got to make a living. Isn't that right boys?" he said, looking to his men for their agreement, but finding little satisfaction. "And a debt's a debt," he persisted.

"What you fail to grasp, captain, is how important a partner the chief is to us."

"Partner? You're calling him a *partner*? Like we're playing card games or something? Listen, that rake's a cheat. I've seen others like him, in every port we've laid anchor. And I haven't cared for a single one of them."

"I'm not the least bit interested in *what* or *who* you care for," said the governor, growing visibly more chafed by this confrontation. "I tell you, he's our partner, and an invaluable one at that. Without him, we wouldn't trade at all. You'd lose your commission. We'd lose the whole damn thing – this encampment, this whole *region* – to the French, or the Dutch, and in a matter of months, or weeks maybe."

"Bah, that's no concern of mine, is it? I'd just as soon tow these bastard slaves for the French as I do for you bloody English."

"What heresy," said the noticeably irate governor. "Young man, I advise you to be careful with that loose tongue of yours."

"What, *this* tongue here?" he replied, wagging it about in front of his crew like the tail of a jumpy dog, hoping without success to elicit laughs. "Nobody's ever complained to me none about this tongue, least of all the ladies," which at last drew a cackled response.

"Wait here," barked the governor, as he tore off toward the main house, leaving the captain baffled as to his own next move.

Governor Marsh left him baking under the scalding sun, made to wait like an errant schoolboy who knew or suspected that some sort of punishment was coming, but incapable of stopping it. While the small band of soldiers looked on, with an almost menacing stare at the sailors they considered to be their inferiors – though their ranks were not comparable – the captain and his men kept themselves distracted. They surveyed the gun wall. They exchanged the kind of lewd jeering with each other intended to provoke the ire of their supercilious and more decorous military counterparts. They made equally lewd nods to the trammeled slaves passing in line, as if somehow it were necessary to accentuate the tyranny of their power over these doleful souls. It was the type of conduct the soldiers professed to find repulsive, but which in truth would not have been unknown to them either, and that continued right up to the moment the governor returned.

"Do you see this?" he asked the captain, wielding a piece of rolled parchment, with traces still visible of the wax that once sealed it, and tied with a rich red ribbon.

"Yeah, what is it?"

Unfolding the document, the governor continued, "It's my orders from the king. *Your* king and mine."

"What of it?"

"He instructs me to ensure the delivery of slaves to the colonies, in quantities his ministers require. And that any and all goods shipped *here* are delivered as ordered, no matter what. He instructs me to use force if I have to."

"Yeah, well, you get your orders from the king. I get my orders from my testy *wife*, and *she* says I'm not to come home 'til I get what's owed me, *no matter what*," he added with more than a hint of ridicule.

But that impertinence was a step too far for the governor, who rolled the parchment back up into a tight coil and then, in one short motion, used it to slap the captain plain across the face.

"You'll surrender that shipment to the chief, or I'll have

you relieved of your command. Do you understand me? What's more, you'll take his second son as agreed back with you to London. And you will treat him, I swear it, with all the courtesies the king's protection affords him. If not, then it's really very straightforward – I'll have you locked up in a cell," he said, with an exclamation that detonated like a mortar shell. "And you'll rot in there, for all I care."

And with that, the governor turned and walked away, leaving Captain Crichton to recover from the pitiless humiliation he'd suffered in front of his men. An ignominy he was powerless to oppose, surrounded as he was by the armed men under the governor's direct rule. Though he desperately wanted the gold to which he believed himself entitled, he knew he was at greater risk of being divested of the one currency even more essential to a ship's captain: his authority.

He was quite unaccustomed to such condescension. The veins in his neck and temples erupted again in a hotheaded rage, as the ghastly contortion of his features once again took hold. And as he walked away, muttering vague obscenities, he left both the soldiers and his own men unnerved by the ugly malice that had returned to his face.

## CHAPTER 8

Keeping to one of the well-trodden, serpentine trails that wound faithfully toward the village, William was walking alone, when suddenly a sprightly young field mouse crossed his path. The four spindly black stripes down its back swayed from side to side in a wave-like movement, to dizzying effect. Its flashy tail, half again as long as its body, convulsed back and forth, as quickly as the flame of a flickering candle. Scurrying from one edge of the footpath to the other, smelling the soil for sorghum or barley seeds, the jittery creature seemed confused, unsure where to turn to next. He scampered over the dirt and into the skirting grass, and then abruptly stopped in his tracks. He opened his dark, bulbous eyes wide and unblinking toward William, with his head cocked upright and utterly inert, as if immobilized by doubt and indecision. As if overcome by the gravity of fear.

William, who stared unflinching back at the mouse, had been in much the same humor for several days already. He too was entirely unsure of himself. Irresolute and unsettled, he too was riddled with doubt and with fear.

One moment he could be profoundly self-assured. Tomorrow he would set off confidently on an audacious journey. To England, this fabled country of kings and courtiers, where he might expect to be treated as an important if eccentric visitor. He would discover for himself what was true about this remote country, and what was mere legend. In doing so, he might even become something of a legend himself.

Then precipitously, and especially in more private moments such as this one, he was consumed by doubts, terrified at being forced into the kind of unknown against which as a child he'd been so amply warned. To William, the unfamiliar had early on become a synonym not for jaunty fun, but for peril. In this at least he'd learned his lessons well. And yet, with the rising of the next day's sun, he was to go. He'd be carried far away from the clutch of his father's villages that had Annamaboe as its center, and that had his father's house as its heart. The house he held so dear, with the spiny straw packed fast on its hard floors, whose roofs leaked so stubbornly, and whose constant riot of activity was the envy of some and the frustration of others, but that was unquestionably the great pride of all.

The house was his academy, his canteen, his dormitory. He'd never received lessons anywhere but in the cramped alcove off its courtyard that crudely served as a schoolroom, and to which a constant series of tutors had briefly taken up their posts. He'd never slept anywhere but in the larger room reserved for the unmarried boys of the family – a place where innumerable plots were hatched, where the petty jealousies and conflicts of youth were launched and where they were almost as quickly resolved.

Just as he knew every inch of the house, he'd come to know every bend of the rich domain over which it ruled. He could anticipate the shadows of the fluttering trees as the sun reached its highest point in the summer sky. He could interpret the music of the rapids, as the river narrowed and curved around every bend. Above all, he knew and he held dear the balmy smell of the land's fine, baked red clay, as if it were a gracious, soft perfume.

William bent down to take some of that scarlet earth in his hands. He breathed in its unique fragrance, then watched as the grist drained slowly through his fingers like sand in an hourglass. Tomorrow he would leave all this, and that leaving would be a torment. He would be separated from this glorious place, from his family, and from his friend Kwame, whom he expected would struggle with bouts of loneliness while he was away.

But William also knew that his friend wouldn't stand still. He would change and mature in this year to come. Kwame would soon see the world differently. He knew from his own experience that a single year could mean the difference between being a credulous boy and a stout-hearted, rugged man. It had happened to him. One day he was carefree; the next, he had responsibilities, or at least expectations. And one day, without warning and without fanfare, he had understood the only thing that had since come to matter to him. Without looking for it, he had found love.

Which is why, most of all, he dreaded the separation from Esi. The bond they'd formed over this past year had proved itself no less than a miracle. It had answered questions neither of them had ever thought to pose. In doing so, their cynicism had become faith, their misgivings had become convictions.

William, who had long thought of the many mawkish stories his English tutors made him read aloud as lies – stories of moonstruck knights and dewy-eyed maidens mourning their absent lovers – had since come to think these contained the only universal truths worth knowing.

And the real miracle was that Esi felt precisely the same way.

Yet, like so many of the lovers depicted in those rose-water tales, heroes whose duty so often called them away, he wavered in the face of his leaving. What would become of Esi? Would she forget him? Would she forsake him for someone stronger? Someone who'd one day be a chief – not just the son of one today, or the brother of another tomorrow? Though he trusted that no new love was ever stronger, their passion for each other hadn't yet been tested. And in every one of those bombastic English stories, it was only by overcoming the most stringent of tests that the sincerity and the tenacity of that love had been proved.

So to leave Esi behind, as he had done only a few moments earlier, was the cruelest challenge of his unpracticed life. It was no solace to him that her anguish was the equal of his own; it only heightened his suffering. The tears he had started to shed so freely burst out from a long-buried place, and from the unbearable weight of anxiety. It would not be the only time today he would know such tears.

Still on the dirt trail, William slowed his pace, hoping that somehow walking more slowly might encourage time to dally as well, and might delay the inevitable moment in which, over his shoulder, he would no longer be able to see his love's faint profile in the distant passage. But Esi had already disappeared below the dimpled pitch of the road he knew so well, and all he could see behind him was the white heat of the horizon. By now, even her tenuous outline had gone from his view.

Kneeling on the path, he stopped to pick up the mouse, not more than a few days old. He caressed its stubbly back as if to comfort the quivery and hungry creature. As if they could comfort each other in this wrenching moment. Then he put the mouse in one of the roomy pockets of his woven shirt, to carry with him as he went to meet Kwame, to whom he'd also need to say a proper farewell.

At least that meeting wouldn't be as fraught as the last one had been.

At least it wouldn't be for William.

\* \*

"What about you?" asked Kwame, "How many have *you* got? I've managed . . . twenty-two, twenty-three, twenty-four. Yes, twenty-four! That's got to be a record. And you?"

"Not as many as all that," replied William. "I've got . . . I've only managed seventeen so far, I think."

Huddled by the side of the road, the friends were counting the small rocks each had amassed in a contest to build the highest and the sturdiest mounds they could engineer. It was the type of contest they'd disputed plenty of times before. They stacked the craggy stones in a way that mimicked how the English soldiers stockpiled their cannon balls, as they might have stacked up slushy snowballs in anticipation of a friendly wintertime attack, if either of them had ever seen snow. Together, they were simply idling away the time until the start of the elaborate events marking William's departure. They were events that would involve every able person in the community, and that would also mark the end of their privileged time alone, not just for today, but for the whole of the year to come.

"Put them on top of each other, like this," said William. "Like a pyramid. It'll be stronger like that."

"Really, you've got nothing to teach me on that point. Mine are piled higher than yours have *ever* been. So I'll do this the way I want to. My way. As a box, as a tower, as a pyramid, who cares. I'll do it how I choose."

"Yes, you're right. I'll never get to twenty-four anyway, that's for sure."

"No. Never."

"So let's note this day well. The day our Kwame won one of our competitions at last!" said William, as he toppled over his mass of stones.

He knew of course that this would be the end of their genial games – their foot-races and bird-spottings and mound-building – and for once, as a parting gift, he wanted his friend to win. But he hadn't really lost the game, he'd lost interest. He was distracted, thinking instead of the enigmatic land to which he would soon be sailing.

And Kwame knew it, too.

"Why are you so bothered, William? I don't think I've ever seen you so... so uneasy. This is such a – such an *incredible* day. The start of an unimaginable journey. The journey of a lifetime. If it were me, I'd be celebrating. I'd be screaming my happiness for everyone to hear."

"But it isn't you who's going, is it? Me, I don't want to go. I don't want to leave this place. At least, I'm not sure I do."

"Don't want to *go*? Why not? Think of everything you'll see. Everything you'll learn. I'd do anything to be able to go with you. Anything. It's an adventure, William. Just the sort of thing that's required for the King of the Endless Sky. The sort of flight we've always talked about."

"That *you've* always talked about, Kwame, not me. For me, it seems so very far away. I don't think you have any idea really just how far England is."

"The farther, the better. You won't get two chances like this."

"And, well, it's all just a mystery, isn't it?" said William. "We don't have any understanding of the risks that lie out there. The evils that might live in that place. Or at least how different it will be from here."

"Nonsense. Different is good. Different is – is exciting!"

"And . . ." William hesitated, "there is one other thing. It's . . . it's just that... it's that I need to tell you something, Kwame."

"What is it?"

"You see, there's also, well, there's a girl."

"A *what*?" he shot back, in pretended astonishment.

"A girl. I've found a girl. And we're in love."

"Ha! That's just foolish. Stupid. Probably the stupidest thing I've ever heard you say. What is love? And what do *you* know about it?"

"I promise you, it's true. I'm as certain I'm in love as I am that you're standing there in front of me."

"She must be a witch then, this girl. She must have cast a spell on you. You might already be doomed."

"No, no, it's not like that. It's not like that at all. It's nothing to be feared. Actually, it's just the opposite. Really, you can't imagine how . . . how magnificent it is. I know, I know, you think the very *idea* of love is pointless. That it's, what did you call it, *foolish*? That it's not worthy of strong men, able men, like you and me. But Kwame, I'm telling you, you're wrong. I was wrong, too. This feeling, this sensation, it just . . . it just makes your heart beat faster. Even thinking about her, I can feel mine beating away, harder. One minute, when she's there beside me, I can feel a kind of burning inside. A fire. A fire unlike any I've ever felt before. The next minute, when's she gone, my heart just freezes. It turns to nothing but ice. And even that cold freeze, that pain and confusion when she's away from me, even that – I'll tell you a secret Kwame, even then – I *like* how it makes me feel. Being in love, it's . . . it's somehow being . . . well, somehow like always being on the edge. Between safety and danger. Between fire and ice. And I like it."

"Humph," shrugged Kwame, unmoved by this declamation.

"And do you know *why* I like it?"

"No, I can't possibly imagine why!"

"It's because I feel needed. Wanted. I feel . . . *loved*, that's what it means to me. No, it's not something to fear, or to run away from, but something you have to run *to*. This feeling, Kwame, it's . . . it's like diving from the cliffs at Bogi Cove. Like falling from them – it can be both scary and exhilarating at the same time. Except that you know you'll land safely. That you'll be caught, each and every time. I feel as if I've been falling all my life. And with her, at last I'm certain there will always be someone there to catch me."

Kwame, who sat stock-still listening to his friend's breathless speech, was little short of flabbergasted by this outpouring of effusive emotion. He couldn't quite believe his ears. He could hardly believe that such gushy prose poured forth from the companion he knew to be so often reticent, so cautious, and that he was able to deliver such a queer, ardent monologue. And he wasn't the least bit impressed by it.

"What silliness. Really, I don't know what to say. Does she have a name, this sorcerer?"

"She's called Esi. And she's no sorcerer. Or if this is a spell, long may it last. If only I had known this spell, this dream, earlier. Because, it *is* like a dream. Because, whatever happened before, I tell you, my life only began when I met her."

This reply was too much for Kwame to bear. As he listened to his friend's fervent discourse, he felt as if every last word pierced through him like a sharpened dagger. Every new avowal of this love was only a denunciation, a negation of the boys' inveterate friendship; the two states were incompatible. William, it seemed, had turned away from their abiding ties, from the unspoken promises and mutual pacts they had made to each other. Promises that seemed to dissipate so easily as to make a mockery of them.

He had already come to suspect this. Many times Kwame had spied the couple in their euphoric outings and secret meetings of rhapsodic intimacy from which he had been barred. But now it was different. Now it was no longer clandestine, but openly divulged. His champion, his idol, had betrayed him. He knew, for he had already heard William defame him as worthless, and today William was standing before him making this blazing, unguarded declaration as if to humiliate him further, and to demean him. His only friend had crumbled against the conjuring of the first girl to present herself to him. Their countless hours, countless days, of both shared idleness and frantic activity, had been sacrificed at the first opportunity, and with it, the bedrock of Kwame's faith had been sacrificed as well. Everything the guileless young man thought to be true, everything he held dear, had just evaporated like an earnest resolution that falls away at the first obstacle. It melted away like that one last, headstrong cloud on a scorching summer's day. Thoroughly injured, Kwame couldn't imagine that his desolation could get any worse, but then William pushed the dagger in further.

"I need you to do something for me," he said.

"Of course," he replied excitedly, keen to reclaim any opportunity to feel wanted. "Just tell me what it is. To keep the canoe in good shape until you return? To make sure your brothers don't steal your things?"

"I need you to . . . to look after her. To look after Esi. Make sure no harm comes to her, even if you have to do so from afar."

"How can I do that, William? I don't even know her. What would you have me do?"

"I don't know exactly. Just . . . just watch over her, that's all. Try to keep her safe while I'm away."

"If that's what you need me to do, I promise, I will," replied Kwame. But he didn't mean it. Even as he nodded in agreement to this unwelcomed request, he seethed with rage and with resentment. For the first time ever – since the earliest days of their friendship – he could hardly wait for this encounter, for one of these sanctified meetings he had once so valued, to end.

\* \*

So well organized was the service at the sacred grove, to which all had assembled to mark William's departure, that it came off as if it were a routine event in the liturgical calendar. The ceremony was almost identical to the one organized in his brother Badu's honor two years prior. But this was only the second time such an observance had taken place; it was only the second time that one of their rank would travel beyond their borders. And this time, it was William who received its favor.

The gifts had already been laid out for his inspection. His sisters had spent the better part of a month weaving him a striking, long-sleeved tunic made in the tribe's characteristic, geometric pattern – alternating vertical and horizontal stripes of black for energy, blue for serenity, and gold for purity. The men had skinned a fox, and with its pelt had made a long coat for him to wear in the cold European winter, which Badu had recommended, having suffered first-hand that continent's piercing chill.

The climax, however, was the marking of William's tattoo. On passing into adulthood, all of the men in the surrounding provinces and tribes had for generations received the same distinctive scarring of three slanted, parallel lines high on each arm. At the bottom of these simple bands, each man also had a more ornate, more fearsome scar carved into his skin: the figure of a leopard, with narrow slits for eyes and fangs, a parade of rounded dots to connote the rosettes on its fur, and a series of strokes arranged in a circle to depict the wild cat's ferocious, open jaw. The execution was simple and looked almost careless, except that each man's was virtually identical.

As always, it was left to one of the priests to make the incisions, which he did with the aid of thorns plucked from an acacia tree. After each deep cut, he smoothed a handful of herbs into the wound to help protect against evil, as well as a thick black paste, ground from the ash of burnt wood, to stop the bleeding. But the principal purpose of the paste was to stain the lesions, to produce a greater contrast with William's dark skin after the healing process was complete.

The cutting of the flesh was agonizing enough; the insertion of the mixture of herbs and charcoal dust made it almost unbearable. Yet William showed no evidence of pain. He knew that to surmount this ordeal without flinching was a sign of profound strength and will. It was also a sign of consideration for the chief, under whose watchful eye the ritual was taking place. Such impassivity bestowed honor and respect on the chief, as well as on the recipient; and even as he was being bathed in praise, above all things William craved his father's respect. Though he hadn't yet done anything for which to feel exultant or boastful, though he hadn't even yet left these blessed shores, with each cut of the thorn he felt more self-satisfied. Every burning prick only gratified him, elevating his standing in his father's hesitant esteem. This progress helped to keep his mind off the pain, as did his stroking of the fidgety field mouse, still hidden in his shirt pocket.

The scarring complete, the ceremony was concluded and the entire company walked as one to the harbor to meet the waiting ship – just as it had done for his brother, but this time with William at its head. At its rear, Kwame followed warily along, dragging his feet. He was dreading what his false-hearted friend's leaving might mean for him, but still eager for the scoundrel to slink away from Annamaboe at last.

While the crowd delighted in the music and the booming cheer, only Kwame noticed that William's attention was elsewhere, frequently looking back behind him. For it was there, in the bleary distance, that William saw Esi, a flimsy silhouette of a lone figure under cover of the thickset vegetation, who stood watching the march as a silent witness. And Kwame, following the line of his friend's deflected stare, saw her too. Like a dark cloud he couldn't quite shake, even here he saw that the interloper had managed to interfere.

This was the supreme blow, and the final confirmation that William cared only about this contemptible girl. It was categorical proof that he was little more than a traitor. A liar. A rat. And with every injurious word he could think of to describe him, Kwame felt the dagger in his chest go in deeper still.

\* \*

"This cabin seems very fine," the chief remarked, having briefly been left unattended with his son on board the *HMS Lady Carolina*. "Quite suitable for a prince. But how do you open this damned window?" he practically shouted, as he struggled to unfasten the latch on the porthole.

"I don't know, Father. Like this, I suppose," said William, but he couldn't get the hinge to budge either.

"You fool, how are you going to make it in their land if you can't do the simplest of things?"

Humiliated, William replied, "Should I ask the captain when he comes back?"

"Yes, you do that. And make sure he brings you everything you're entitled to. Everything due to someone of your rank."

In fact, the stateroom allocated to him was small but very well-appointed. There were feather pillows piled high on the hefty bed, over crisp white cotton sheets, and a plentiful quantity of candles to light the room at night. Next to the bed stood a pair of sparkling drinking glasses with an exquisite diamond pattern in the crystal, and a matching decanter for wine or for water held ingeniously in place by recessed holes of just the right size carved into the rich wood. It all presented the inexperienced traveler with far more luxury than even the chief could have envisaged.

"Before that blasted captain gets here, whatever his name is . . ."

"Crichton. David Crichton."

"Before he gets here, your Captain Crichton, remember

just one thing, son: do me proud, like your brother did before you. Come home with my name, with my fortune, greater than when you left."

"Of course, Father."

"And beware these people, these English. I've dealt with them for years, and I know they are not to be trusted."

"But they've been good to you, Father, haven't they? They've been good to us."

"They've done what is right by us. Not because they've wanted to, but because they had to, and because we've never given them the choice. Never forget, we have the advantage. We have *always* had the advantage. They need us more than we need them. And never, *never* let them get the better of you. You, William, are the son of a chief. And the Fante are a great people, a powerful people."

"I will make you proud, Father."

And then, in the most generous words he had ever heard his frosty father say to him, the chief muttered in return, "I know you will, son. I know you will."

And with that, his father was gone. He descended the ship's gangplank, rejoining the retreating revelers who had marched all this way in the searing heat to see the valiant young man on his way. Because the ship would remain in port until the early morning – when the next high-tide would lift her off the pier and guide her into the open sea – William could hear the celebrations for some time yet, as the crowd noisily made its way back up the steep climb to the chief's house.

Kwame, however, stayed behind. He took his place on the nearby hillside where so often the pair of friends had marveled at the unbroken convoy of ships as they entered port. This evening, as the light began to fail, and with the aid of the binoculars William had left behind for him, he fixed his gaze on the *Lady Carolina*. If he was glad to see his one-time friend finally boarded, he would be even more relieved if he could confirm for himself that the faithless hypocrite had actually gone.

So he waited. He waited patiently, and he watched, as the men readied the ship for departure. He watched as they scrubbed down her topsides one final time, unfurled the headsail on the main mast, and threw overboard the scraps of food and refuse they had no intention of hauling all the way across the Atlantic.

And that's when he saw it. When, from the portside of the main deck, a group of a half-dozen bruising men, each wielding a weapon of some kind – a knife, a whip, a copper pipe – surfaced in a kind of spontaneous configuration, huddling in front of the cabin where William was still settling in. And then, in an instant, they rushed into that cabin, a moment later dragging their startled passenger out by the thick shock of his black hair. With a fat, frayed piece of rope, they tied William's hands behind his back, and pushed him to his knees. Then, they too waited.

Captain Crichton soon arrived. From this distance, Kwame couldn't make out any of what the captain was saying. He couldn't pick up a single word of the invective he was spewing in William's direction. Words that, could he have heard them, would have made clear the extent of the captain's wrath at having been swindled by this upstart's presumptuous father, at the loss of no less than ten guineas, and at the further outrage of having been made to ferry that thief's son to London, as if he were a person of some import. As if this African boy were a person at all. For Crichton, this was more than any self-respecting captain could let pass. He would take his revenge on the chief, on Governor Marsh, and on anyone else who might be dumb enough to oppose him. The gold he was owed might not be repaid, but here at sea at least he would win a moral triumph, and a famous one at that, to reclaim his stained reputation, not least among his own men.

Even from the far-off spot from where Kwame watched the scene, the villainy of the captain's intentions was clear enough; it became unmistakable as the captain took what looked like an iron bar from one of his officers, and used it to strike William in the stomach. Again and again, savagely, until he fell prostrate to the ground in agony. And even then, the beating continued.

With the captain still looking on – his usual distorted expression morphing into a more wry, perverted grin – he ordered the first mate to shave William's head. He did so bluntly, with a cooking knife that left him hemorrhaging and the blood then seeping down his face. The crew then stripped him of his clothes – the ceremonial tunic his sisters had only just finished sewing for him and his draw-string trousers – and threw those clothes over the side. They poked at his still raw tattoo, as if to provoke and bring to heel the truculent leopard it was meant to depict. And with his arms still tied behind him, they took him naked down below to the galleys. They pushed him down the last few crooked steps, and out of Kwame's field of view.

William stumbled over the arms and legs of the other men. There were so many men, he couldn't possibly make out their number. They were so solidly packed that their dense mass swallowed up the few columns of light that managed to slip through the unbending planks. He was chained up next to other prisoners, with the noise of the tightening bindings ricocheting uncomfortably off the arched walls. That terrible noise broke the eerie quiet that reigned – not so much a silence as a constant throb of low sighs and groans, like lumbering whispers that permeated the airless space.

On the hillside, Kwame remained quiet as well. He said nothing. He did nothing. Dispassionately, and with full intent, and right up to the moment the light failed, he simply watched the scene unfold. Hadn't he been hit time and again by his father? Didn't he know what it was like to feel the cold thud of metal striking his back, his belly, his head? For all of his blood that had been spilled by his father's hand, for all of those tyrannical thrashings he'd endured, he'd come to believe the fierce accusations that accompanied them. No matter how groundless, no matter how far-fetched, he'd been made to believe that the fault was always his. That he had somehow, unknowingly but undeniably, brought that ruthless punishment upon himself. And so it was for his friend. William had proven himself to be unfaithful; he had revealed himself as false, and the gods had chosen to punish him for it. And as he walked home that evening, Kwame could only find a kind of satisfaction, a justice in that.

Early the next morning, he awoke even more certain that the penalty inflicted on William was nothing short of divine retribution. He needed to be taught this lesson. To be taught, before his return in a year's time, how to be a more humble, a more solicitous friend. And so as the *Lady Carolina* finally began to quit the shore, having untethered herself from the moorings that had kept her steadfastly in place for the two short days of her visit, Kwame prepared coolly for his morning's chores. He prepared as well for his lessons – the tiresome sums and English exercises – that for the first time would be held without his friend, without his accomplice, beside him. He did so with an untroubled heart.

On board the ship, however, and from the start of the furious assault that yesterday had seen the passenger dragged out on deck, the tiny field mouse had stayed hidden under the generous bed. In all that great commotion, the door to the newly vacated cabin had slammed firmly shut, leaving him trapped and frightened by the thunderous racket around him. But in the morning, with the first abrupt pitch of the ship away from the pier, the cabin door slid open at last, and with it the mouse gathered his courage. He attempted his escape. He scuttled across the main deck and ran onto the gangway just as it was being pulled up from the quay. With only moments to spare, the shivering creature jumped to safety, his feet once again returning to the shore.

William would not be as lucky. Like the untold thousands who went before him, and the thousands more who would follow, his feet were unlikely ever to return to the fine red, perfumed clay of Africa.

# PART TWO

*Esi,*
*Hunter of Crocodiles*

*You may choose to look the other way,*
*but you can never say again that you did not know.*

From a speech before the House of Commons
William Wilberforce (1791)

# • CHAPTER 9 •

The younger boys seemed to revel as much in tearing down the exuberant decorations as their sisters had done in assembling them. For many months now the house had been adorned with wreaths of gossamer feathers, with tooth-edged cowrie shells and gilded pieces of glass beads. But even these lavish garlands paled in comparison to the copious amount of red sweet-berries raided from the crowded shrubs abutting much of the property. Row upon row of the fleshy fruit had been strung up on coiled twine of un-combed cotton, like a succession of brilliant ruby necklaces. The glimmering strands were hung over the fire-pit in a half-moon arrangement; they were hung too on the lintel beams over the doorways, drooping just low enough for the women to brush them lightly as they passed underneath, as if doing so could confer good fortune, though there was no established superstition or Fante tradition to support this. These broken bursts of color cloaked the main courtyard in a kind of whimsy. They lent the many monochrome spaces a sense of renewal, and a flash of infectious life in the otherwise dull enclosure.

Yet with the chief's consent, that life was today being extinguished, much more handily than it had been created. The boys ripped down the trimmings with abandon, one after the other, in swift movements that bordered on violence. They trampled on the shells, they stomped on the berries, all in an exaggerated way to demonstrate their authority over nature itself – all the more facetious as they had little authority, little consideration anywhere else in the strict hierarchy of Chief Eno Kurentsi's busy home. Until their coming of age, they enjoyed hardly any consideration at all. So they exulted in their flitting act of destruction, grinding the crushed juice of the berries into each other's faces and bare chests as if it were war paint.

This might have been a lighthearted moment of distraction for the boys, but in this they were alone; no one else in the household was inclined to be celebratory. Certainly not any of the adults. Over the course of the week just past, yet another wave of English and Dutch ships had made port. They brought with them the furious activity that accompanied every landing. Their arrival also brought the conventional bonanza for the local men – the wages and tips for unloading and loading of cargo and, for the more enterprising among them, the bribes and thefts that were rampant. But nowhere was there any sign of their beloved. Nowhere was there any trace of William.

And soon the rains would come. Soon the seas – already becoming rough in a foretaste of much greater disturbances to follow – would be too tempestuous for any vessel to sail, regardless of how competent was her crew or how sturdy her construction. From today there would be no more ships calling at Annamaboe until the end of the rainy season. There would be no more hope that William would make it home before then.

It had been more than three years. Three years without any word from William directly or news of his whereabouts from his English hosts. And the absence of news, as much as his physical absence, cast a dull gloom over the uneasy household.

Not that it slowed the perpetual churn. The constant purr of chores and housecraft kept the place as orderly as its doyenne Adwoa expected, and as irreproachable as the hypercritical chief required. The family went through its paces, with long months of punishingly familiar routine and with vanishing moments of surprise. With times of both great joy and those of stinging sorrow that together are the lifeblood of any home, but all of it obscured by the absence of their second son, and with a weight that hung over them all like gravity: heavy, invisible and pervasive.

Few felt the weight more than Chief Kurentsi. For three years he'd been pestering the English for news of his son, increasingly frustrated by their lack of interest and piqued by their hubris. Prodded by the village elders, goaded on by Eukobah and the other wives, he took every opportunity at his regular meetings with the governor to berate him for information and for action. He made repeated shows of amassing his men in front of the fort, of spoiling a measure of the soldiers' supplies, of openly flirting on occasion with the rival French commanders. But in all that time, he always stopped just short of threatening the English, for the chief knew he was in a weak negotiating position; he knew he had as much if not more to lose than did his longstanding partners. After all, he might ultimately conclude a comparable alliance with the French or the Dutch, whose predatory forces were nursing their huge ambitions not far down river. But if the English had proved nettlesome as allies, they would be doubly so as opponents. Not least, over the decades of their uninterrupted occupation, the squatters had come to understand the intricacies of the chief's lands, and the strengths and vulnerabilities of his forces.

And though he'd never confess it to his people, he understood well enough the risk that, with more firepower and more resolve, they could overwhelm the Fante. Today the chief was the middleman, supplying captives to insatiable foreign traders; tomorrow, it could just as easily be his own people who ended up enslaved.

Even more than the chief, Esi too felt the heavy burden of William being away. William had told her their reuniting would only be a matter of time, and that the hours, the weeks, might pass slowly. That along the way there might well be many a lonely mile traveled, but that those hours, those weeks, would pass. He told her, too, that his homecoming would be finer for it.

But time without him was proving no friend; before long it had become the enemy. And that enemy was no longer idle, for by then it was suiting up for warfare. Each passing month meant she only matured further, and maturity meant settling down. And settling down could mean only one thing: marriage.

Plans were afoot for Esi to wed. First it was just shrinking mentions she thought she'd overheard. Quiet murmurs she caught about a local boy she'd seen but once, who'd come to visit with a small escort from a nearby village on an ordinary summer's day. That day, there was an unusual amount of fuss in the normally starchy home, though she had thought little of it. She paid it no heed. She definitely paid no heed to the boy. He was tall and gaunt, and not unpleasant to the eye, but he was quite ordinary. He was drab and tame, and devoid of the self-confidence she admired most; the very traits she so valued in William. By contrast, this meek, withdrawn boy scarcely spoke a word, and avoided meeting her stare. She wouldn't have been able to pick him out of a crowd, if by chance she had come upon him on market day.

Those early quiet mutterings, however, had lately turned to more frank proclamations. Her parents had taken to talking openly with visitors of her marriage. She learned that the priests were being consulted for a date, and that the chief was being consulted to set a bride-price. And in all of this, no one stopped to take account of her. No one thought even to inform her, which was just as well, since her parents would have been gravely angered by her opposition and doubly scandalized to learn of her reason for it.

As the relentless march toward that fated day became ever closer, Esi became increasingly alarmed. So today, just as she'd done every day for more than a week, she waited in front of the chief's house. Even as the boys annihilated the ribbons and streamers inside, she sat motionless outside the house, without a precise objective in mind or a clear plan of action. She sat there detached, crouched in the charred dust as it swirled in the spiraling winds announcing the coming storms.

She studied the house. She memorized its uneven lines and the difference in the patina of the mud walls between where the bricks had been sun-dried and where they'd been baked. She considered the uncountable threadlike fractures in the clay plaster, or where bits of mortar and straw peaked out from the poorly sealed joints. When the swarm of chickens that seemed to have unquestioned jurisdiction over the yard engaged in one of their cacophonous brawls, kicking up even more of the gritty dirt in their wake, she barely flinched, and just stared at the house with an unremitting, redoubtable intensity.

What was she expecting? That William, as if by some miracle, would suddenly emerge from the house to enfold her in his muscular arms? That, failing that, the gods would send some propitious sign of his welfare and of his approaching return? All she hoped for, all she knew, was that something decisive needed to happen. That something meaningful would need to change. That the unbearable circumstances to which she had so long been condemned, the total ignorance of William's fate, would have to come to an end. And in this, she was certain of only one thing: only she could make it so.

She had almost given up faith. So Esi was more than a little astounded when William's mother emerged that morning from the house, crossing the yard past the quarreling chickens, and walked right up to her.

"I know, dear," said Eukobah to the startled girl. "I miss him, too."

"But – what? But how could you *know*?"

"A mother knows, dear. She knows all. I saw you at the leaving ceremony, there in the distance. I saw you at the far end of the pier as we waved goodbye to my son. Who else had he been sneaking around for? Inventing reasons to go to the market. Stealing food from our kitchen. Paying attention like never before to his own appearance, his head always floating somewhere in the clouds."

"So all this time, you . . .?"

"Not all this time, but yes, I understood. I saw the change in his behavior. In his moods. I told myself – that could only be love. Remember, I'm not so old as to have forgotten these things for myself, or not to be able to see them in others."

"I am . . . I'm Esi," she said nervously.

"Yes, dear, I know that as well. I am Eukobah," she said, taking the girl's hand in her own palm, with a soft touch that telegraphed an immediate familiarity. "Truth be told, I'm worried about him, too."

"What could have happened to him? What's become of him?"

"I don't know," replied Eukobah. "Really I don't. We simply can't know."

"Do you think he's forgotten us? That he's decided he wants to stay in England, with all the advantages there must be in such a place?"

"Forgotten us? Oh no! The poor boy must be thinking of nothing else."

"Well, I'll tell you then what I'm afraid of: that he's found another girl out there. A girl who maybe is prettier than me, smarter than me, richer than my family could ever be."

"Oh, I don't think even *you* believe that to be true," said Eukobah. "That can't be what your heart is telling you. It's not what mine is telling me."

"No, you're right. Of course you're right. I don't know many things, but one thing I *do* know is that he wouldn't leave me for another girl. But . . . so, what then? What is keeping him away?"

"I wish I knew, Esi. Truly, I wish I did."

"We must ask the governor. He'll have answers. We must insist to the governor that they send him back. That he send William back to us. It's been so long already, what else can they teach him there?"

"The governor? He's a very frightful man. I don't think he'd be very helpful to us."

"So then, we must ask the chief to go see him. Why hasn't he gone *already*? After all, it's *his* son," said the girl falteringly, still shaky from the shock of this unexpected meeting.

"The chief, my husband – he's afraid to. He won't admit it, not to you or to me or to anyone, but he's afraid to confront the governor."

"Afraid? What can a man like that fear?"

"He fears for his power. His authority rests on less than you think. If Eno . . . if the chief upsets the English, if he provokes them, they might just stop their gifts and their funds. At least, that's what he dreads the most. It would leave him poorer, yes, but more important, it would leave him vulnerable."

"Vulnerable to what?" asked Esi, taken aback by this response.

"To all *sorts* of things, actually. Things that you and I can't possibly understand. Power is a mystery as much as it is a weapon."

"Well then, *I* will go. *I* am not afraid. And what have I to lose anyway?"

"What madness," said the older woman, "it would be absurd."

"Why *shouldn't* I go?"

"Well, to begin with, the chief wouldn't permit such a thing. Never."

"We could convince him, you and me. I suspect you're able to convince him of just about anything, when you put your mind to it."

"That may well be true, but even I have my limits. He would never allow it. He wouldn't allow anyone but himself to deal with the governor, least of all the women. The chief won't change who he is. You know, dear – however long the bamboo stays in the water, it will never be a crocodile."

"Well, I won't tell him. I simply won't tell the chief I'm going."

"That would change nothing, and it would only infuriate the chief when he learns of it later, which of course he will. Because, dear, the governor wouldn't tell you anything. No, he won't help you. He wouldn't even agree to see you in the first place."

"I'll *make* him see me," exclaimed Esi. "I won't leave the fort until he does."

"My sweet girl, you wouldn't even make it past the gate!"

But Esi was as persistent as she was rebellious, and was determined to have her way. And Eukobah knew it. She admired it. She saw much of herself in the girl's gutsy resolve. She knew as well that the girl's confrontation with the governor – just as William had said to Esi of their reuniting – would only be a matter of time.

* *

On the morning that followed, Eukobah once again crossed the great length of the yard in front of the house to rejoin Esi. This time, she didn't come with empty hands; she brought with her a small, simple meal of cornbread and jams to share with the girl. For several hours they talked of many things, of anything but William, as if by some tacit accommodation. They talked of their predictions for the coming harvest, of how fair was the smell of the just bloomed but already pendulous white flowers of the margosas. And slowly, assuredly, as the time passed, they managed to build an ever-greater trust. They were building a fellowship, brought close by their common concern for the lack of information about William's well-being, if not about how to remedy it.

On the day after that, it wasn't only a meal that Eukobah brought with her, she brought Adwoa as well, and so the small gathering expanded from two to three. And soon enough there were even more. Another wife. Another sister.

Before long they had become six, then seven, then eight. An impromptu sisterhood that was a welcome relief to Esi, despite the slightly ticklish questioning that followed.

"Tell us about William," said Adwoa. "Anything you like. Tell us, for instance, about how you fell in love."

"Oh yes, dear," chimed in Eukobah. "Tell us that."

"I couldn't possibly do such a thing!" replied a visibly flustered Esi. "Not in front of . . . not in front of his mother anyway. I *am* sorry, Eukobah."

"Trust me," said Adwoa, "if you talk about him, he'll be with us. We will feel his presence."

"But it's too . . . too personal. Too intimate. Even with my own sisters, if I had been lucky enough to have had any, I couldn't talk about such things."

"Your own sisters? But *we* are your sisters," said Eukobah. "Adwoa, why don't you go first, to show Esi how it's done? Talk to her, remind us all about when *you* were first in love. Talk to us about when you first saw Eno. When you first met him."

"Well, I was in awe, I can tell you that. I was . . . speechless. Yes, speechless for once, if you can believe it," to which many of the girls giggled, never having seen Adwoa at a loss for words. "I was so afraid, and so excited at the same time. I mean, he was going to be a chief. A chief! What an honor, I thought, to marry such a man. But what fear, too. And his hands! Such big, amazing hands. You see, I spied on him before I met him. I never told anyone, but I stole into his village, this village, one morning to see him before the wedding, to get a good look at him. I recall telling my mother afterward, in tears, that I thought he might . . . that he might strangle me, and that I wouldn't marry him. I wouldn't marry that man! And yes, on our first night together I was so completely terrified when he first went to touch me. I was shaking, I can still remember it today. But that didn't last long. Not long at all. I remember that, too. It was wonderful. His touch made me feel truly alive, maybe for the first time. It was, let's be honest sisters, it really *was* wonderful."

The wives who had known such things for themselves nodded in agreement; the younger girls, who didn't yet know of such wonders, who thought of marriage and physical intimacy with a mixture of both fright and inflamed contemplation, could only manage a nervous, awkward laugh.

"So tell us, Esi," said Eukobah, "why William? What drew you to my son?"

"No really, I can't say. Not like this."

"Sure you can," Eukobah replied, whipping up the other women to help goad Esi on.

"Well, alright then. What can I say? Is he the ideal man? No, probably not. He has these dents, these pockmarks on his face, I don't know what from. They're like deep creases. And he has this raspy, croaky voice that I tease him about, as if he sounds like a sickly frog. He hates those pockmarks, and he hates his raspy voice. And I don't love William *despite* these flaws, I love him *because* of them. Because of his imperfections. All the silly little things he dislikes in himself, I love about him."

"You see, it's as if he's here," said Eukobah. "I can already feel him among us."

"I knew you would," replied Adwoa, casting a broad smile in the direction of her friend. "I knew we all would."

But Esi, who had started to think about, to whisper about her love – who but a moment ago was reluctant to engage – could not any longer be halted, surprising the women and thrilling the girls.

"I feel him, too. But then again, he is *always* with me.

He is everything to me. Sometimes late at night, when I lie very still in my bed with nothing but the stars to keep me company – when the rest of the house is sleeping around me – I find myself thinking about him. And I imagine, I'm sure, there and then, that he's thinking about me as well. And then, like the flashing stars in the night sky, he just fills my head. His face, his playful laugh, those rugged, forceful hands that used to hold me so tight – they're with me in the nighttime, as they are in the day. Everywhere I go, I can't avoid him, even if I had wanted to. All day, every day, I find myself trying to make sure I memorize things I've seen, unusual and startling things I've heard – a bruised nestling chick being looked after by its mother, a terrifying stroke of lightning cracking just over the roof of the Englishman's church – so I can tell William, so I can share these things with him when he returns. But memories of him can be hard, too. They can be very bitter. So many of the things I see when I'm out walking – the paths we went down together, the warm stream where we used to like to swim – it brings me . . . today it brings me nothing but . . . nothing but pain."

Here she stopped short, overcome by her own storytelling, by the lucid imagery she had herself evoked. And as she rose to take momentary leave of the women, to regain her lost composure and to dab away the salty tears, she left the younger of her newfound sisters in a state of wild admiration. They could only dream of such love. Their dreams were only ever of such things.

Eukobah, clapping the dirt from her hands, stood up to join her, to help ease Esi, and to warn her.

"Yes, we have to try to find William. But you . . . *you* mustn't seek out the governor, my dear. It's too risky. Let us find another way."

"There is no other way. What choice do I have?" asked Esi. "What choice is left me but to do *whatever* I can to bring some peace back? To bring our William back. If the chief will not help us, if the gods will not help us, then we must help ourselves."

"The gods would forgive you such an act; I'm not certain the chief would."

"And still, I will go."

"Yes, I guessed that's what you'd say. In your position, I'd likely have said the same. I suspect I'd have done the same thing as you're planning to do." Taking the girl's hand in her own once again, Eukobah continued, "But please then, please take this one gift with you. It might just help," she said, presenting Esi with a small object, the size and shape of a beached pebble.

The item might have been modest in size, but its value was infinitely greater than any pebble, and Esi knew it straightaway, for it was an uneven but luminous nugget of gold. It was heavier than she would have thought. The scintillating lump of metal was almost the size of her thumb, and she thought its shape resembled that of an ostrich, with a long shank for a neck and a swollen bulge for a body. The whole rumpled chunk was covered in fissures and cavities that had been eroded then polished by the local riverbed from which it had been recovered. Smooth and cool to the touch, it seemed to carry a tight concentration of sunlight within it as firmly as a locket holds a sacred relic.

"Where did you get *that?*" asked a startled Esi.

"Never you mind that. A woman always has her ways. Use this if you need to. But only *if* you need to. Use it to get your way into the fort, and as influence with the governor. Reason and flattery can only get you so far with men. Money and wealth are what they're *really* after. Money can take you much further than any charm or cunning could hope to do."

Even as Esi examined the glinting object, Eukobah signaled for the other women to join them. One by one, each of them came forward to hand over a similar gift. None of the nuggets they offered was as big as the first, and some were no larger than the shattered cowrie shells that had come to litter the courtyard, but they were all impressive just the same. And by the end, Esi had in her possession a handful of gold more valuable than any hoard she could have imagined. She had a small leather purse from Adwoa as well, to carry this unimaginable treasure.

"Dispense with this gold carefully – it's the only advantage you have," continued Eukobah. "And fill the bottom of this small bag with stones. Make them think you have even more of these nuggets than you do. A woman must always give the impression she *has* more, *sees* more, *knows* more than she really does. Then go, with our blessing," she said, as she, then in turn each of the women, kissed Esi on the forehead, clasped tightly her hand – expressing their empathy and their support in every way they knew how.

Not another word was spoken; there was nothing left to be said. After more than a week of camping in front of the chief's house, Esi left the compound at last. Waving until the last moment, she left her sisters behind. They were fine, charitable women but strangers to her still, and who, she was well aware, might just as easily have proven adversaries.

All afternoon and all of that evening, she sat by herself on the ridge above the swimming hole that was one of her lover's favorite hideaways, marveling at the serendipitous blessing of meeting these women. She felt for the first time since William sailed for London more than three years ago that she was not friendless. That others too – many others, it seemed – shared her concerns, shared her sadness at the young man's continuing separation. These were friends whose spirit, whose invincible force, would accompany her like stiff ammunition into the battle to come. She marveled, too, at the priceless trove she'd been entrusted by these kindly women to assist her in that battle, stroking the tiny pieces of gold for luck as if they held divination within them. As if they possessed occult powers, strong enough to overcome the huge challenges she knew her bid to see the governor would generate.

So when she set off early the following morning – before the sluggish sun had time to show its face and the warbling crows had time to loosen their congested lungs – she did so with supreme determination. She deliberately chose a direct, unobstructed path, and one that would not hide her progress, but broadcast it. She walked straight through the heart of her own village, and the many others that lay between her starting point and the coast. Along the way, she hardly noticed how dry the fields of corn and palm were. She gave no thought to the swelling river as she walked alongside it, a river that within days would burst its banks in the barbarous storms already bringing both exalted life and gratuitous destruction to the neighboring valleys. And in the half day's walk to the sea, not once did she allow herself to imagine how terrible might be the last leg of the journey, the long walk up the steep ramp of the fort to meet the English governor. Despite her solitude, despite the remarkably slight figure she cut against such a theatrical landscape and against such cursed odds, she could not be diverted.

She wouldn't be alone for long, for by then, word of her quest had started to trickle out. News spread of the brave if foolhardy crusade she was undertaking. And when she'd come close to the furthermost limits of the chief's empire – when the last of the flattened dirt path surrendered back into its earthen tomb – there sitting by the roadside was a solitary man. An unassuming, stalwart young man, dressed in threadbare clothes and with frayed leather sandals on his calloused feet. There, waiting for her, sat Kwame.

## CHAPTER 10

"What's your plan?" asked Kwame.

"What do you mean, what's my *plan*? I'm going to see the governor," replied Esi. "To tell him we want William back. But you know that. Isn't that why you've come all this way with me?"

"Yes, of course. I meant, what's your *specific* plan? We can't just walk into the English fort and ask for an audience with the governor. He's not likely to agree on the spot like that to meet with us, a couple of local kids he's never set eyes on before."

"Maybe. Maybe not. But we have to try. We've come this far already."

"We need a strategy," he continued. "To agree on an approach. And that's just about getting in to meet with him in the *first* place. Then I guess we need to figure out what to tell him. What to ask him. Have you thought this through?" He spoke with an assurance and an authority that belied his youth and his total inexperience in such matters. It was an authority that surprised even himself.

The pair were sitting together in the custodial shade of a majestic sycamore-fig tree, under the canopy of its sprawling limbs. Around them were hundreds of kindred trees, which differed from each other only slightly, in the girth of their trunks and in the braided curves of those limbs. These ancient hardwoods stood like foot-soldiers in advance of a well-disciplined army. They formed the extreme boundary of the swirling forest that flanked Annamaboe. Behind the two young travelers stood this vast, dense, mystical orchard; in front lay nothing but the immense English fortification that was the target of their long walk. Across the broad plain, the shapeless boulder that towered over the land had finally come squarely into view. Over the years this glowering stronghold had been the subject of much discussion, and much conjecture, among the villagers. Esi and Kwame alike had often wondered about the intrigue and chicanery it must have accommodated. It was undoubtedly the theater for countless encounters just as hazardous as their own promised to be. An encounter about which both felt more than a little unsettled.

"I don't really have a plan, I suppose," said Esi. "Except to talk from my heart."

"But you'll get nowhere. To begin with, you'd need to know their language. And as far as I can tell, you don't know more than a few words."

"How many words can it take? They'll understand. The governor will understand."

"Esi, you need – *we* need – a better idea than that. A more definite idea. And you're going to need me, I can see that plainly enough. I can negotiate with them. Argue with them if I have to. I can speak their language, and I can talk to them as men talk to one another. But I think we need to prepare better. We need more time. Why don't we come back tomorrow? We can bring more people with us then, too. If you cross a river in a crowd, my mother says, the crocodile won't eat you. Tomorrow we could bring some of the chief's men, to help convince the governor that we won't accept anything but satisfaction."

"No," cried Esi, "it must be today. I have no more patience. I have no more time. We can't wait one day longer."

"What's another day? He's been gone for three years. And . . . and, aren't you the slightest bit nervous? Afraid to confront the English all by yourself? All by ourselves, anyway, just the two of us?"

"No, I am not afraid. I'm not afraid of anything anymore," she said, picking up a cracked, buff-green fig that had fallen before its time and from which the desiccated seeds had begun to take flight. "When I was a child, I was frightened of just about everything – of whatever was unfamiliar, of the dark, the sounds in the night, the night itself. And worst of all? I didn't have anyone to talk to about it. No one to share my anxieties and the gloomy visions I sometimes had. I kept those visions to myself. I didn't have the benefit of brothers or sisters, the kinds of friends I could trust enough to ask for sympathy. It was . . . it was almost like I had no speech. No voice. You have to understand, in my father's house, I was expected to observe and to obey, but I wasn't expected to participate. From the first day I could talk, I was told to keep quiet and to listen. And so I did. I would listen to stories, plenty of scary ones, about mysterious things that skulked in the night, and about evil spirits, especially about those that lived in this shadowy forest. These stories filled me with terror. I heard about our tribesmen being lost to those spirits. From a safe distance I could often see for myself a hint of odd creatures in the thicket, whose form I couldn't quite make out, and that terrified me all the more because of it. And I could hear for myself the strange, horrible howling sounds like weeping that came from far inside the bush. I wouldn't go near it, not for anything. Not, that is, until I met William. I remember the first time William and I were alone, and when all of a sudden we came upon these same woods. He took my hand, anxious to lead me in. I could see how excited he was to take me into the heart of this place. So imagine how surprised, how disappointed he was to learn that I wouldn't dare step inside. That I was scared of the blackness. To me, even the flakes of bark I could see on the ground – bark like this, gnarled and discolored – were like signs of death. But William, he showed me how to see it in another way. To see *many* things in other ways. To him, the cast-off skin of the sycamores shouldn't be confused for weakness or for death, but rather as a sign of growth, and of health. 'These monuments,' he likes to say, 'were born before us, and they will outlive us.' To him, the strange sounds and the unseen creatures here are our friends. And he says that if you look closely enough, you can see signs of welcome everywhere. Signs of protection, as if every seedling and every shrub is watching over us. They keep us cool and dry, and they keep us hidden from prying eyes. Mostly, he's shown me that I needn't be afraid. He, too, has been there to protect me. He's sung songs to soothe me. Beautiful songs I can still remember. I remember him saying that, one day, the wind itself will sing to us. That the twisted branches will bow down as we walk by them, in a sign of their blessing. Since then, I've spent so many hours staring into this forest, making plans for the two of us, thinking about our future. But I'm still waiting for that song of the wind. I'm still waiting for those branches to bow down."

"And now?" asked Kwame.

"And now – now I am no longer afraid. My worries, my uneasiness, all that dissolved with him. They melted away with the first kiss from William. Maybe, Kwame, I still haven't seen many things in my life and in my time; maybe you haven't either. But I do know that, all I'll ever remember about my life is everything about my life with him. He's allowed me to see not the *dangers* but the beauty of this forest, of the unknown. He's shown me that happiness is possible. He's even given me that voice I dreamed of, and the chance for everything else to be as I dreamed it would be. Today I don't have to imagine love or happiness, Kwame, because I've seen what it looks like. It is William singing his beautiful songs to me. It's being alone with him in this wood, without fear. No, it's not fear that cripples me anymore, it's grief. These days, the happy songs are gone. And once again, I haven't been able to share any of this. To talk about it. That voice he helped me to find has deserted me again. With William away, it's as if I've been living in a world without sound. Until only *yesterday*, when the women of your village opened their hearts to me, I've had to bear this like some kind of private shame, bottling up this pain, this sorrow inside of me. Alone."

"You're not alone anymore."

"Maybe. But it still feels . . . well, empty. Raw. You know, Kwame, I'll tell you a secret. Earlier this year I saw a woman in my village, a young woman not much older than me, lose her husband to the fever sickness. All of us watched as he became too weak to move. In a matter of weeks, he became delirious. And when the life was finally taken from him, I saw everyone uniting to console this poor woman. But what I *really* felt, most of all, wasn't sadness, it was envy."

"Envy?" he replied, startled.

"Yes, envy. Because, although maybe it's selfish or maybe it's mean of me to equate William's long parting with this woman's terrible bereavement, the real difference is that I haven't been able to, I haven't dared talk of *my* suffering, of *my* grief. There's been no one to rally around me like those who rallied behind my neighbor. Even when those neighbors talk of other things, when they talk of joy, this talk escapes me. I hear the other girls telling of their romancing, of their expectations of marriage, and I can't, I won't participate in that either. Mine has become a lonely, dreary life. And all this heartache, it's changed me. Truly. I'm afraid that William, if he were to see me today, might not recognize me, the woman I see when I look in the glass. This woman is not nearly as carefree or as sunny as she used to be. Above all, he'll see that I've lost my confidence. This cannot go on, Kwame, not for one day longer. I will not lack confidence anymore. No, I will not be afraid anymore."

\* \*

The pair walked across the long, barren tract to the fort, as slowly as a river slopes its way downward for miles toward the plundering sea, and just as inevitably. Kwame could see that she needed more time to gather her final thoughts for the contest ahead. He needed time as well, if only just a few minutes more, to get a stronger hold on his courage. Neither dared speak for fear of breaking the other's concentration, for each was lost in a personal deliberation about the unknowable jeopardy in store, the staggering range of plausible scenarios, and the different approaches they could take to the coming confrontation. But like the tributaries of a drowsy river that fork along the way but end up bleeding into the same ocean, so too the divergent schemes and devices Esi and Kwame were contemplating would lead them both to the same inescapable point. To news of William and a pathway to bring their prince, their friend, their future home.

Esi looked on with a mixture of wonder and dread at the mighty garrison. The structure, much larger than any other she'd ever seen, had risen very nearly on top of the old one that had itself, and for generations, become an indelible feature of the coastline. To Kwame it seemed to have doubled in size since the last time he'd gotten this close to it, when several years before he and William had accompanied the chief on his first interview with the then new governor. Its size achieved exactly the intended effect: to intimidate both those who arrived as invited guests, and especially those who pondered the odds of arriving as aggressors. Not that anyone could confuse the two young callers today as potential aggressors. To any soldier standing watch, they would at worst be seen as harmless trespassers, like bothersome flies one simply swats away from a bountiful banquet table.

The enormity of the construction didn't deter Esi, but it did cause her to hesitate. When not more than a few hundred steps away, she offered Kwame a tortured half-smile, as if to reassure her younger companion. She needed plenty of reassurance herself.

It wasn't only the dimensions of the building that gave her pause; it was also its muscularity and the permanence this implied. The fort had an organic air about it, as if it had arisen on this very spot by nature's express command. As if, like the land on which it stood and from which it miraculously emerged, it had always been there and always would be. Where one side of the sleek, blindingly-white limestone edifice seemed to emerge from the fathomless waters, the other, landward side seemed to materialize right out of the hill that hosted it. It was fronted by ramparts cut directly into the native scabrous rock, the sodden earth forming an unalterable part of the walls themselves. These walls leaned cautiously upward to a great elevation, and sank low again into the sandy ditch below that had been cut out in front, and which only amplified the illusion of height.

The ditch was meant to be filled with water, as yet another impediment to intruders, but the engineers hadn't managed to finish the job before they left for more prestigious commissions, or for less risky ones. It had quickly filled up with long weeds and unruly dandelions. It looked almost inviting. For a while at least it might easily have been mistaken for a children's playground in any common English park, though no child would have been unwise enough to play his leapfrog or his ball games here. But the widest section of that deep trench – the one that had the misfortunate to find itself just under the kitchen windows – had been filled high with rubbish. Decaying corpses of half-eaten animals competed with paper wrappings of imported sweets and all manner of other refuse that no one in the household cared enough to cart away. If anything, it was indicative of the lack of discipline Governor Marsh had inherited, and which he had never quite managed to reverse.

The four lookout towers at cardinal points, on which cannon and poised guns had been mounted, hadn't fared much better. Protruding outward so the guards could observe the walls on either side, the grainy stone on the towers had weathered quickly, eroded by the salted air that constantly assaulted it. Worse still, the slate shingles on the rooftops, affixed by a battery of the chief's men for derisory wages, had been poorly placed; unsurprisingly, given that the men's training in this grueling craft was desultory and brief. Many of the tiles were dispatched by each new season's first great storm, as soon as the irascible wind announced itself. These too ended their service ignominiously strewn across the half-finished channel.

Work to repair the towers and the roofs had been abandoned for lack of funds and lack of interest. Governor Marsh would have written to his superiors in Whitehall to complain about it, if only he had bothered to maintain the fiction that anyone in London actually read his letters and his reports. He'd soon realized that complaints were effortlessly rejected when they weren't outright ignored. It was, after all, implicit in the simple, unbendable code of the Crown Service, and fundamental to the endurance of the Empire: make the most of the adverse conditions left to you, extract whatever you can for king and country, and leave the place no worse than you found it. And Governor Marsh had found the place both relatively peaceful and hugely profitable.

When at last, in the early evening, the visitors arrived at the base of the fort, the blunt heat had started to slacken. They could feel the cool night air roll its way softly off the side of the hill. The rogue flower buds that abutted the fort's pedestal were closing their blooms for the night. The birds began to retire as well, and brought to an end their dulcet chirping, as if they had run out of things to say.

As they approached the dingy gate house, they saw a lone sentry standing watch. The two studied this curious figure as if he were an alien species, though his uniformed kind had long been a pervasive presence in the land, threatening trouble, if rarely actually causing any, and vaunting unchallengeable control like some sort of usurper gods. At least they seemed to think of themselves as such. They had built a baronial temple of rock and earth in which to worship and to assert their illicit power. A power they exercised over freedom or captivity, over life or death, as if it were their sovereign gift.

But this characterless species before them was no god; like the gate house he commanded, he was untidy and bedraggled. His standard-issue black leather boots were covered in a layer of dust so thick, it was as if he'd done battle with a storming column of sand, and had lost. Convincingly. He seemed greatly harried by his uniform – tugging at its buckram collar, shifting the gun looped over his shoulder from side to side, unable to find a comfortable place for it to rest. His bloodshot eyes communicated only fatigue and tedium, as if he had just invented boredom and had wanted to claim it as his own. He was clearly more interested in examining the blade of straw he held between his rotted teeth than in surveying the land for infiltrators.

As the visitors stared at the guard, he stared right back at them, with just as much stupefaction and incredulity. His reaction suggested that perhaps no one had ever dared to confront him on post before. And given the audacity of it, for all Esi and Kwame knew, maybe no one had.

All during their advance, Kwame had been preparing. He would deepen his voice, in order to convey strength and maturity – an idea that came to him as he crossed the dusty field. He would puff out his chest, thinking it would make him look bigger, like a wide-winged macaw strutting its tail feathers. But his newly assumed low voice didn't quite match his lean build, and the effort required to puff out his chest left him breathless and unsteady. He risked tipping over if he maintained the stance for much longer. Next to him, Esi remained unaffected and unmoved. She stood not behind him, but beside him, as if to say, we are equals, we are one, and we are stronger because of it.

The soldier, however, wasn't the least bit impressed by

this show of unity and force. Indeed, he hardly seemed interested at all. "Yeah?" he said, "What do you two want? You lost?"

"We want to see the governor," replied Kwame with a feigned coolness, in the note-perfect English he'd learned in the schoolhouse but which he had hardly ever practiced beyond those narrow walls. He hoped only that his lessons wouldn't fail him in this first and decisive test.

"You *what?*" shot back the soldier.

"We want to see the governor."

"That's what I thought you said. Wanted to make sure I got that right. What you want to see him about, then? You lookin' for work? A handout? Maybe a medal?"

"Our fren inlan," said Esi, in a garbled approximation of the words Kwame had rehearsed with her only an hour or so ago.

"What did she say?"

"Our *friend* is in *England*," he corrected the embarrassed girl.

"Got a friend in England, do you?" said the guard. "Who's that then? The Chancellor of the Exchequer? The Lord Mayor? No, wait, wait, let me guess, it's the Archbishop of Canterbury, isn't it?"

Oblivious to this brand of sarcasm, Kwame continued undeterred. "No," he said, "he's the son of Chief Eno. His second son. William is his name. And he's gone to London, on one of your tall ships."

"The chief's son, is it? Nope, never heard a word about 'im."

"But the governor has. The governor knows him, and he knows where to find him. How to arrange to send him home."

"Why'd he want to come back here then, your friend,

if he's holed up in England? Trust me, things is much better there than in this dank swamp. I'd give more than a few shilling to be there meself." Having worked out by her clutched expressions that Esi must be the missing boy's sweetheart, he added insidiously, "And probably found himself a nice girl or two there as well, I'd bet. No shortage of nice girls, obliging girls in England, that much I can tell you," he added with a lascivious wink.

This last remark Kwame didn't bother to translate, but from the soldier's crude gestures Esi worked most of it out for herself.

"Anyway," he continued, "you're wasting your time. The governor's away. Can't you see, the Union flag ain't flyin'. Everyone knows, that's the sign. From George's own palace in Kensington to the loneliest bastion in Somaliland, we don't fly the King's Colors when the master's away. He's off inspecting the barracks down river at Ejubo or somewhere. Probably inspecting the ladies down there, too, if you ask me!"

"We whet," attempted Esi.

"You're wet? What the hell is *that* supposed to mean?"

"We will *wait*," Kwame clarified. "We can wait until the governor returns."

"Not here you ain't. Not on my watch, anyway. He won't be back 'til morning, so I'm told, and that's only if the mules cooperate. So you two urchins go away. Go crawl back into the jungle you came out of, before I make you," he bellowed, brandishing his rifle and waving it about in their direction in a pulsing flourish as if it were a butcher's knife or a samurai's sword.

The swinging of his gun did exactly what the soldier had meant it to do. It gave them both enough of a scare that, instinctively, each took a small step back, then several more. Soon enough, they had reversed clear away, out of any danger, if ever there really had been any.

Kwame's heart was nevertheless still racing. He had prepared for a confrontation, only to be stymied at the first hurdle. For the sake of his honor, he would have argued further, though he understood almost immediately that further squabbling was futile. The governor whom they sought, the one person who might provide the redress they were seeking, was many miles away. And though he could practically hear the kindled blood still pumping in his temples, Kwame was clear-headed enough to know that his energy was best saved for a protest that actually mattered, when eventually it came.

And so, despite preparing all day for this moment, he would have to wait until morning to get what he came for. Esi, too, had been preparing, but for much, much longer. For weeks, for months. For as long as she thought she could bear. But she, too, would have to bear it a little longer yet.

By the time they'd returned to the edge of the wood, they had resigned themselves to spend the night around the warmth of a makeshift campfire, once more within the sanctuary of the forest that once had so frightened Esi. They had only the meager supplies she'd brought along to sustain them, and those rations would have to be divided in half.

And then something wondrous happened.

Without noticing and without trying, they each came to understand that they were no longer suspicious of each other, and that they needn't think of the other as a rival, for they had become allies. They had almost become friends. Friends who had shared their first real trial, a meal, and a warm fire. Above all, they shared a mission that was close to sacred for them both. Without expressly discussing it or even pausing to acknowledge it, they'd come to realize that the one thing missing from each of their lives was the one thing that united them, and that separately had brought both of them to this fateful campaign. They realized, too, that they were on the verge, tantalizingly close, of accomplishing what they had set out to achieve, and that tomorrow would see the start of an unstoppable chain of events that would inevitably end in William returning home.

So they rejoiced. They allowed themselves a moment of release, and a moment of welcome levity.

Kwame took the lead. Emerging after a few moments from behind the largest nearby trunk, he exclaimed in a curious, indeterminate accent, "What do you want, children?" The singed leaves on his head had been shaped to look like the English soldier's cap. Combined with the stick he slung over his left shoulder like a musket, it left little doubt as to the character he had assumed. His movements were as stiff as if he were wearing the guard's taut uniform. "The governor's not here, I said! Can't you see? The flag is not flying over the roof. Which flag you say? Why, the Union flag of course. What, are you blind?" swallowing his words under the grass between his teeth, as if it were the soldier's droopy piece of straw.

"We will . . ." stuttered Esi.

"You will *what*?" he continued. "I can't hear a word you're saying!"

"We will . . . oh, what's the word?... we will *wait*," replied Esi, able now to deride her own halting contribution to the interview with the guard.

"Yes, wait. Wait here, I tell you . . ." said Kwame, as he disappeared again behind the thick column, only to emerge moments later for another faultless impersonation. Once again, there was little doubt as to the object of his efforts:

this time, it was to be the governor himself. He made use of the same crumbly leaves, stuffing his shirtfront to simulate the growing paunch that lately everywhere preceded the king's representative in Annamaboe, and whose steady expansion – like the testimonial rings on a cross-section of a tree – had accurately marked the three indolent years he'd already spent in his post. He walked directly toward his audience, picking dementedly at the lapels of his pseudo uniform, as if it were awash with specks of dust or inundated with fruit flies, in a bid to parody the commander's notorious reputation for meticulous dress.

"I've been down at Ejubo, I have," intoned Kwame. "I'm not sure how this sorry lot of soldiers managed to keep this fort standing while I was gone. Not too sure how *I* manage to keep standing, for that matter," he joked, leaning over precariously, as if his bulging belly would at any moment cause him to fall. "I've been inspecting the cattle. Been inspecting the ladies, too. They sure have some fine cattle down there!" which set Esi off into another aching fit of giggles.

"Alright, it's my turn!" she said, setting off behind the massive tree. As she did so, as she worked to prepare a disguise as clever as his had been, Kwame spoke to her. He almost had to shout so she could hear.

"You know, Esi, you know . . . we needn't be worried. Tomorrow, this will be easier. Our entry, I mean. Tomorrow we'll know what we're dealing with. I wish we'd been more successful with this first meeting today with the guard, but it's not important. What matters is that it'll help me prepare, it will help *us* better prepare. The next time, tomorrow, we won't hesitate. We know we'll be up against this fool, or someone just like him, and that we can deal well enough with him. I won't back down. I won't be intimidated."

"Nor will I," she said, from behind the bristly curtain.

"Good," he only had to say, as they understood each other well. Anxious for Esi to reappear, he hesitated briefly before continuing, "Be warned, I'm coming back there..."

"Don't you dare!" she shrieked, moments later coming into view. With limp flowers set clumsily in her hair and a mess of leaves spilling out of her comically enhanced bosom, it was clear as a blue sky whom she had targeted: the governor's wife. Whenever she had seen Abigail Marsh, whenever either had seen her – at the market, at the port – they couldn't help but remark on the fact that her thick tresses bristled with flowery exuberance, that her bouncy velvet and silk dresses were utterly unsuitable for the tropical climate, and so at odds with the simple modesty with which the local women tended to adorn themselves. Esi didn't have to utter a word, to attempt to lampoon the language or the farcical mannerisms of the governor's wife; Kwame had already doubled over from laughter.

Their amusements continued well into the evening. As the time flattened before them, Kwame pointed out to Esi the constellations in the midnight sky, or at least those he was fairly certain he could pass off as having recognized. He taught her some of the secrets of how to play at stacking stones, just as William had taught him. And as they tired, they helped each other forge beds from the clammy soil and from the leaves that hours before had been integral props for their cheeky costumes.

By the time the light had all but faded, Esi had settled into an acute sense of calm. She no longer felt any of the lingering jitters she would anyway have been loath to admit. She knew only cheerfulness and composure, and a patent faith that this night, so unexpectedly, would be the first of many to afford such blessings. In the nighttime stillness, she came to believe that she could feel signs of hope, of encouragement, all around her. That the governor would see reason when confronted with it. That he would intervene to help tear William away from the studies or the amusements or whatever else it was that was keeping him so long in England. If she strained her ears, she could almost hear the song of the wind that had been promised her, and she settled into a restive sleep under the shelter of this familiar forest, in the kind of restrained calm she had only been able to pine for these many months.

Kwame, by contrast, couldn't find sleep at all. For all of his brassy confidence, he was kept awake by his persistent uncertainty about the outcome of this enterprise that he still thought rash and chancy. But mostly, he was bedeviled by a growing impression of remorse, and of shame. It was a slow, ruthful recognition that he might personally be to blame for the sorry predicament Esi found herself in, and that William found himself in, whatever and wherever that might be. It was this same remorse that had driven him to join Esi, to wait for her earlier by the side of the path. These were pangs of conscience that he'd only lately begun to question and to understand. He alone was not so certain that his friend, his accomplice, had ended up staying in England of his own free will, or even that England was where his friend's trumpeted journey had ended. He alone had seen what had befallen William on the deck of the *Lady Carolina*, the terrible violence and humiliation inflicted on the unwary traveler. It was violence that might well have been within Kwame's power to interrupt, if not to prevent, and about which he had chosen to do nothing. His was a craven act that, increasingly, he couldn't help but see as a sin of omission, as damning as if he had wielded the iron bar or whip himself.

And so, as he continued to peer at the chasm of the night sky, he looked out not for constellations, nor for the branches around him to bow down, but for his own, pressing signs of hope. Signs of forgiveness. For any sign at all.

## • CHAPTER 11 •

Nothing brought greater joy to Abigail Marsh, greater relief from what she considered the wretched adversity of her
husband's current posting, than tending to her angel-wing
begonias. Their dazzling flower heads – in creamy pinks,
in smoldering reds and oranges – were her one consolation.
She cultivated a jumble of these cherished plants in special
decorative pots, positioned judiciously around the long balcony outside the couple's bedroom window. They offered
a bracing touch of color against the drab, deeply-fissured
stucco of the fort's exterior walls and the clay-colored spindles and stone plinths of the balustrade. Not least, the ceramic pots and thick, latticed stems of the plants hid many
of the unsightly cracks in those spindle rods. Cracks that,
to Abigail, were the very embodiment of the fort's shoddy
construction, and emblematic of everything that was wrong
or wanting with this unhappy place.

Today, however, not even the flowers could help to
shake her low spirits. Never far from distress, today she felt
on the verge of despair. It needn't have been this way.

Her one goal for the morning had been to arrange the
kind of simple lunch her husband would enjoy – that he
would expect – as he completed the tiring journey back
from his tour of Ejubo. She had instructed the cook to

prepare only the most rustic of meals, consisting mainly of a pea soup and a fresh loaf of bread.

She knew precisely how the hurried meal would unfold: he would eat his soup in near complete silence, and as he finished, he'd break off a piece of the bread, and make a show of soaking up the scraps from the bottom of the bowl, where he said the flavor was always most intense. In truth, it was his way of giving effect to the Protestant ethic of thrift he held so dear. As if to say, nothing in my household will go to waste, and that here, frugality must be seen as a grace, on par with hard work and diligence.

Abigail braved this invariable ritual stoically and with great patience. Her only pleasure in it was when Thomas would pause to admire the willow or butterfly pattern at the bottom of the ornamental porcelain bowls, and to compliment his wife on having the discernment to choose such a pleasing pattern. He would look at it as if it were his first time seeing it, though he had repeated this exercise hundreds of times before. Not once did Abigail tire of this gentle artifice.

Nothing could have been more uncomplicated than the basic menu she had planned for today. After all, it didn't require the use of any of her new-fangled implements; there would be no need for the mechanized spit for roasting beef or wild game, or the icing spatula for cakes and the other confectionaries she liked so well. The cook wouldn't need to synchronize the timing of any elaborate recipes, as Abigail sometimes did in her youth by reciting the Lord's Prayer a set number of times.

The new girl, however, was hopeless. By this time she'd been in their employ for the better part of a week, and still she seemed bested by her duties. She'd been recruited hastily, since her predecessor had left so suddenly, without explanation, and at the worst possible time, when Abigail had fallen ill with fever. The sickness had lasted for several tortured days, in which the governor's wife almost completely lost her appetite, and was too unsteady to get out of bed. She'd been too shaky even to tend to her beloved begonias, many of which suffered irreparably from her short-lived neglect. Her infirmity had left Thomas to fend for himself. To engage directly with the cleaner about the washing, with the houseboys for supplies and for so many of the other domestic arrangements, and with the cook to choose and to oversee the menus. She couldn't be sure which irritated Thomas more: having to supervise these chores or being oblivious of how to do them well.

And so it proved with his dealings with the previous cook, with whom her husband had clearly had some sort of row. Thomas, she thought, might have lost his patience with the young, doltish girl. Maybe he'd so lost his temper with her, she felt she had no choice but to leave. Regardless, he'd been so out of kilter about it, he refused even to discuss the incident with his wife. The poor dear, she thought, with all of his official duties, he had quite enough of a burden to bear already!

The cook's replacement, the third since their time in Annamaboe, had been swiftly found. She was operating under a kind of probation, but it was clear she wouldn't last long, for although she might know how to prepare many of the local dishes – to pound cassava into an unappetizing pulp or over-boil shrimps and snails – she hadn't the first idea how to prepare meals satisfactory to an Englishman's palate. And Abigail was staunchly determined to see this kind of refinement maintained in her household, despite the unrelenting obstacles.

For one thing, the girl hadn't chosen fresh ingredients

for today's soup. The peas she used were dried and had been stored in the cellars for months, so had lost their essence. She hadn't simmered them in chicken or meat stock, but in water, so the garlic and the onion were over-powering, as was her liberal use of raw green chilies, which made for a fiery mix, when just a dash of pepper would have sufficed.

To make matters worse, Abigail had wanted to serve her husband a doughy loaf of bread, much like the French baguettes she could find in any local bakery back at home. But the girl didn't know to mix ale in with the flour and eggs, so that the yeast could properly ferment. The result left her not with soft bread but with something more akin to hard biscuits. It was bread that might have been more appropriate to accompany any of Abigail's favorite cheeses at the end of the meal, if any edible cheeses had been available, which of course they weren't.

To top it off, the table settings, too, were wrong. Tea-spoons had been laid for the soup, a fish knife to cut the bread. Even the linen napkins were placed to the right of the bowls rather than to the left, though she had explained the proper way to do this numerous times. And so she brooded. She'd only just managed to repair the settings by the time her husband entered the dining room and sat down for his meal. The soup and bread, however, were un-salvageable. At least he was kind enough not to say a word about it.

Outside the house, Esi and Kwame would have been happy with such pungent, lumpy soup, since a night in the forest had left them hungry. Their rations were exhausted and, though both resourceful, neither was equipped to find adequate sustenance in such an alien environment, so that by the time they arrived at the gate house, they were both lacking in stamina. What they didn't lack, however, was resolve.

There they found a new guard on post, and one who had clearly been warned by the soldier he'd relieved of their likely return. Better groomed than his sloppy predecessor, he would show himself to be equally standoffish.

"You the two who want to see the governor?" he asked crustily as they approached.

"Yes we are," said Kwame, taking charge as they had planned. "We're determined to see him."

"Determined are you? *Determined!* Well, I'm not sure I can allow it."

"Why not?" replied Kwame, with a look that communicated both consternation and conviction.

"He's a busy man, the governor. Not sure he's got the time for the likes of you two."

"But we have important matters to discuss."

"Important?" shrugged the guard. "I doubt that very much."

"Important to us, anyway," retorted Kwame. "Serious enough for us to have come all this way."

"That's hardly a reason for me to disturb the great man, is it?"

"It's not just serious," protested Kwame. "It's also urgent. He'll want to see us, I'm sure of that. *We're* sure of that."

"Listen here, what's important to you, what's urgent to you, isn't likely to be of any interest to a man such as the governor. A first-rate man at that. You can't have any idea of the things he has to take care of every day, the decisions he has to make, all day long. Hell, *I* can't really imagine it. I know *all* about why you want to see him. All about your friend who's gotten himself to England, and that you're fixin' to get him to come home. And I can tell you, this isn't going to move the governor much. It certainly doesn't move me."

It took the visitors a while to work out that this was not some sort of campaign to shut them out, to keep them away from their fated interview with the governor; it was in fact a negotiation. It was Esi who first realized that the soldier in front of them was expecting, and awaiting, an offer. A bribe.

"Kwame . . ." she said.

"Not now."

"Kwame," she insisted, "give him this." She nudged one of the smaller gold nuggets she was carrying into his hand, reminding him that they'd worked out this precise scenario in advance.

He quickly understood, and picked up the argument without losing his stride. "Maybe what we have to say isn't very important to you, or even to the governor, but it will certainly be worth his while. And maybe this will help?" he said, waving the gold piece in front of the soldier.

"Well, would you look at that! What a fine specimen that is." Taking it off Kwame, he bit down on the gold to verify its purity, like a prospector checking to see if it left teeth marks, though he hadn't any idea how to verify or estimate its value. "Got any more like it?" he continued.

"One or two. Which we're prepared to hand over to you and to the governor if he agrees to see us."

As he said this, Kwame pointed to the weighty bag in Esi's hand, more than half-filled with worthless pebbles, just as Eukobah had suggested, but whose top layer of precious metal glistened in the blazing sunshine. The soldier's eyes immediately lit up like gunpowder, working out for himself the share he'd get as a reward for procuring this prize. As predicted, the temptation proved irresistible.

"Yes, I reckon that might help," he said. "Come with me," and in an impulsive and imprudent move – punishable in a better disciplined outfit by a week or more in the stockade – the soldier deserted his post, personally leading the two visitors up the long ramp toward the main buildings.

The path was not a smooth one, since much of the paving had been poorly laid, and many of the cobblestones jutted out dangerously. The sharp-cornered stones often caused the horses and mules, burdened with heavy supplies, to slip in the rain, and the young travelers' unaccustomed feet were likewise unsteady. But though the upswept walkway wasn't level, it was as straight as the bristles on a broom, and it rose vertiginously. The higher they went, the more formidable the whole scene appeared to Esi and Kwame; the more clearly they knew, as well, that there would be no turning back. Studying the high interior walls and the second lines of defense, Kwame trembled with quiet misgivings about what the chief would say when he found out about their wildcat expedition, as he was bound to do. Esi by contrast had no such doubts; she trembled with increasing excitement, in anticipation of William's impending return.

As they came upon the level plaza at the top of the ramp, suddenly the visitors saw what so far had been invisible and unimaginable to them: a hub of industry that clashed with the silent and staid image which, from afar, the colossal building projected. It was more like a workshop than a citadel. Soldiers by the dozen were practicing drills, cleaning their stash of weapons, preparing and consuming improvised meals in the few shady shelters the courtyard provided. Women hired from the nearby villages were noisily pounding clean the soldiers' uniforms, stacking and re-stacking firewood, plucking feathers from the barely-dead chicken carcasses scattered on the ground. The mealy gravel itself seemed agitated, in sympathy with all the assiduous activity taking place around it.

Looking out from this great height, across the infinite volume of the forest from which they had earlier emerged, only then did the pair understand the true scale of the site. And only then did they understand their insignificance within it, an impression of inconsequence magnified by their instruction to wait unattended in the courtyard amidst all the commotion. They were left to sit unceremoniously in the exposed heat, as the soldier sought out the governor.

The corporal entered the main house. Informed of his superior's whereabouts, he promptly climbed the double height of stairs that led to the Marsh's private quarters. He found them in the dining room, and knocked hard on the door to announce himself.

"Enter," called out the governor, from behind that heavy door.

"Sorry to bother you, sir. May I have a word?"

"Really, can't you see man, I'm having my lunch."

"I beg your pardon, sir."

"It's to my wife you should excuse yourself, soldier."

"Yes," he said to her apologetically, "I *am* most sorry for the interruption, ma'am. Please forgive me. I'll come back later, shall I?"

"You've interrupted us now," replied the governor, in reality relieved by the disruption. "So what is it? Whatever is the matter?"

"If I could address you in confidence, sir."

"Well, alright then. I'm sorry dear. I won't be a moment."

"Oh, it's no bother, Thomas," she replied, privately so annoyed that she purposefully violated the convention which normally would have deterred her from using her husband's Christian name in front of an enlisted man. "I'll keep this warm," she said, rising to envelop the soup in the woven tea-cozy the new cook had mistaken for a tureen cover.

"So what is it, man? What misadventure is it this time?"

"There's a couple of locals in the courtyard, sir. They say they want to see you."

"Locals? What locals? Who are they? And why are you bothering *me* with this trivia?"

"They're Fante, sir. Neither seems to be of any significance."

"I am confused, soldier. Why then would I see them? What is this all about?"

"It seems they know the chief's son. The one I believe Captain Crichton took away to study in England. And they want information about him. And sir, they have gold."

"*Gold?*" repeated the governor. "You sure of that?"

"Yes, sir. Here's a piece they've shown me. It's the pure article. The girl, she's got a bag full of the stuff."

"Girl? There's a girl?"

"A young man and a girl, sir. Neither can have seen their twentieth year yet. They're sitting down there in the courtyard, where I left them," he said, as he drew the governor's attention to the hallway window from where he could see the visitors sweltering below in the midday sun.

"I see. She has more of this gold, you say?"

"Yes sir, easily ten times this amount in that bag of hers, I'd say. It clatters like a box of broken glass."

"Right," said the governor, taking a moment to consider his options, looking down again at the lonely figures in the plaza. "The young man, he can wait where he is. I won't deal with that patsy. He looks excitable. He looks like a troublemaker to me. But I *will* see the girl. Send her to the Hutch and I'll deal with her shortly. In the meantime, I'm determined to finish my lunch," he said, turning abruptly to return to the dining room.

The soldier just had time to see a glimpse of Abigail's angelic smile, as she rose to take the ill-fitting cozy off the soup bowl before the door closed again and excluded the couple from his view.

* *

Esi was standing alone by the sash window, peering out into the garish sunlight, when she heard the sharp, rhythmic footsteps. It was a sound that seemed to be gathering pace as it grew louder, and that drifted down toward the pits below where hundreds of pitiable slaves were languishing in rooms whose terrible contents she hadn't appreciated, or even suspected.

As the governor entered the small, austere room, he stood for a moment completely still, like a wax statue or a sitter posing for a portrait. It was as if he wanted to give the girl time to assess him fully and to acknowledge his strength and his power. It gave him time, too, to appraise the girl.

Until that very moment, Esi had been supremely confident in her mission and in its success. She had been fearless, audacious. But as soon as he shut the door behind him, when they stood starkly alone, that mettle started to drain away. Her willful courage and her nerve eroded as quickly as her heart was now beating, humbled in the face of the officer's extravagant uniform, the medals on his chest whose significance she couldn't even have guessed at, the towering physicality she hadn't anticipated. It shrank further still as he moved in closer, into the heart of the cramped room.

He laid down on the desk the papers he was carrying, then took off his heavy jacket, draping it over the single chair. Slowly, he unhooked the bayonet knife from his white belt, then unhooked the belt itself, laying both objects on the desk as well. And then he sat, motionless and expressionless, staring at her with a look so cold it might have come up from a tomb. When at last he broke the agonizing silence, his voice was just as cold as his glare.

"What have we here?"

She had no words. No courage remained.

"So, speak girl," he blurted out.

Still, she found no voice.

"Speak, damn it! They tell me you have gold?" Grasping from her vacant expression that she didn't understand, he repeated, "Gold!" making an exaggerated gesture with his hands to simulate the jingling of coins.

"Yes, gold," she just managed to say. "For William. For send friend William home." She had practiced this construction all night with Kwame, and she delivered it well enough.

"Well . . . let me *see* it. Show me."

She took the leather pouch from her pocket, and let it drop on the desk with a thud. From it, she took out the first nugget she'd been given, the heavy one she thought looked like the neck and body of an ostrich, and she laid it bare for the governor to admire.

"Now we're getting somewhere," he said, grinning as he weighed the polished nugget in his hand. "Wouldn't you know it, that damn soldier was right: seems like the pure thing to me. As do you, too, my sweet. Pure as a kiss from an angel."

He looked her up and down, as if he were sizing up the chances of a thoroughbred horse before a derby. He whispered vague, bawdy phrases for his own pleasure only, punctuating his sentences with a sinister grin that confused her as much as it unsettled her. And all the while she felt his invidious stare on her body with a growing sense of embarrassment and discomfort. As he rose and advanced toward her, Esi instinctively recoiled, edging nearer the window.

"Shy, are we?" he said. "Well, let's loosen you up a little, shall we?" as he reached out to touch her hair.

She winced, and in a swift gesture, brushed away his hand. It was a dismissive gesture that only amused the aroused governor, and that only encouraged him.

"As I thought, shy. I can sort that out, I'm sure," he said.

This time, he didn't wait for her rebuff, grabbing hard a great clump of her hair with one hand. "You just relax now, child, I won't be long. You *do* want to see your friend again, don't you?" Waving his other hand back and forth in front of her, he jabbed her constantly as she struggled to pull away. And then – without warning and without provocation – he slapped her violently across the face, his wedding band lashing her cheek.

Esi fell to her knees, numb, panicked. Unable to communicate her protest in words, she began – faintly, almost imperceptibly – to sob. He paid it no mind. Pulling her up by the tresses of her hair, the governor slammed her against the wall. Pinned against it, he undid his breeches and slid off the stiff collar of his shirt.

"Oh yes, cry, my girl," he said. "Cry out loud if you want to. No one will hear you. No one would care if they could."

Esi jerked her way free from his tight grip and vaulted to the far side of the desk, trying to keep it – to keep anything – between herself and the governor. To create a barrier to thwart the lecherous intentions she had too well understood. And still he persisted, the pert grin on his face hinting that he was reveling in the chase.

As he came around toward her, and as she danced again around the desk, she wasn't just thinking about how to dissuade him of these odious intentions, but how to escape from the suffocating room. She needed a rapid escape from a situation that had disintegrated at breakneck speed, and from which she would need to save not only herself, but also recover the pouch of gold. It was the only bargaining chip she possessed, and she would not give it up easily. Without it, where would that leave her? With no leverage, no influence to use afterward in pleading her case for William's return?

Racing back to the opposite side of the desk, she reached across its warped surface to snatch the purse. But he was quicker, and caught her. Twisting her around, he wrapped his stout fingers around the nape of her neck, as if to choke her.

Esi resisted. She kicked at his shins and pounded on his chest, to no effect. Short of breath, disoriented, she wrestled against him with everything she could muster, all the while battling, lunging blindly to get hold of the leather bag. As her hand skimmed the top of the desk, it couldn't quite reach as far as the gold. But instead, she fumbled onto the handle of the knife, whose exposed blade was as shiny as the buttons on the Englishman's red coat still wrapped around the battered chair. She picked up the dagger and, without a moment's hesitation, she sprung forward to strike him. She pierced his skin with the very first hysterical swing of the blade, gouging his right arm, from which liberal amounts of blood began to flow, covering his white cotton shirt with stains as red as ripe beets.

"Bitch," he cried. "You'll pay for this!"

But in the brief moment he took to turn his head, to look after his oozing wound, she grabbed hold of the gold and ran to the door, turning the handle faster than time, and then bounding up the broken staircase into the light.

"Stop her," shouted the governor, holding his bleeding arm, "the bitch cut me. She's *cut* me!"

The whole of the courtyard ceased its busy labor, and stared at the young woman as she emerged from the Hutch. Esi stared back at them, darting her eyes across the square, searching for someone to assist her, for someone to protect her. Searching for a way out. She looked into the faces of the startled village women, and caught a fleeting sight of Kwame, who shared their surprise and their fright, before a group of soldiers charged toward her. She ran around them as she had run around the governor's desk, like a child in a circle game. But she knew they were too numerous, too fast to out-run, and that some of them were armed. She concluded that the only chance she possibly could have to avoid being apprehended was to take refuge in the large structure in front of her: the main house, where maybe the soldiers would be less likely to follow.

And so she rushed into the house. Instinctively, to get as much distance between herself and the belligerent mob, she bolted up the steep staircase that was the main feature of the entry. On the landing at the top, she was immediately confronted with a series of closed doors. Each one was alike, none revealing the slightest clue about what lay behind it and whether it might offer sanctuary or peril, fortune or misfortune. She would have to choose. And so she elected the door that was farthest away, at the end of the long paneled hallway.

It would prove to be the Marsh's bedroom, in which Abigail was sitting in her armchair, reading again her most recent letters from home.

The governor's wife was more dumbfounded than frightened, and she dropped her correspondence on the floor around her. The two women looked at each other in wonder, almost with a kind of curiosity. Abigail would have liked to ask for, to demand, an explanation; Esi would have liked to ask for help. But there would be no time, no opportunity for the women to exchange anything other than a few confused glances, for by then the soldiers had reached the landing.

Assembled outside the bedroom, they broke their tight formation to make way for the governor. As Esi saw him again, still clutching his wound, she felt trapped, like a fox in a pit. She locked her eyes on him, as slowly she backed away toward the open French doors from which a vigorous breeze had entered, scattering Abigail's correspondence. She lost her footing briefly, stumbling over an awkwardly placed footstool, as she backed out onto the long balcony where earlier Abigail had been looking after her potted plants. And still the governor, surrounded by his men, came closer, shouting grotesque obscenities at her, not a word of which she could understand, though their precise meaning was immaterial; his frothing mouth and blaring voice made their meaning clear enough. She pushed one hand out in front of her, as if to warn the men to stay back, while she placed her other hand, the whole weight of her quivering body, against the narrow, rickety railing. As she did, one of the moulded spindles cracked under the weight. And then another. And then, at once, the whole balustrade collapsed.

From far below, Kwame tried to cry out, to offer some sort of warning, but it was already too late. Everyone in the bustling courtyard was witness to Esi's fall. It could be heard as far away as the thickest stretch of the forest, where once she had been promised that the wind itself would sing her a blessing, and where she had discovered love. But today, the wind changed direction. It rang out not in songs of blessing for her, but in lamentations.

# PART THREE

# Kwame,
# King of the Infinite Seas

*I have been driven many times upon my knees by the*
*overwhelming conviction that I had nowhere else to go.*

From '*The Second Battle of Bull Run*'
Abraham Lincoln (1862)

# • CHAPTER 12 •

Those who knew masonry best stood at the head of the long chain of men, pouring layer upon layer of the damp mud they were being fed into the hole. The sizable hole in the wall that, not an hour earlier, they had themselves sliced open. They slathered the mud onto the tangled thatch of twigs, reeds and straw they'd already kneaded into every obstinate crevice. Rocks and cracked shells had been thrown into the mix to bulk it up even further, then the whole soggy pile was glazed with a thick coat of manure, to ensure that the breach was tightly closed and that the seal would hold fast.

Now that Esi's lifeless body had been carried out of the family house – not through the door but, as tradition dictated, through the opening in the wall – the men took care to close it again quickly. They'd taken care as well to remove the corpse feet first, so that the soles pointed away from the house. As they marched toward the burial site, with the body already three days cold, they dropped sticks and thorns along the way in an irregular, zigzag pattern that could only confuse her spirit, exactly as they intended. For the men, her kinsmen, knew perfectly well that the deceased girl depended on their service to guide her, to speed her to her eternal destination, but they also wanted to make certain her spirit wouldn't one day be able to find its way back.

All morning Abenaa, the girl's mother, had stayed composed as she looked on, and as the men put the final touches on the muddy seal. She offered the masons and those farther back in the chain refreshment from the rising heat. She even lent a hand in preparing the grout. But once the body was gone, she stayed back, alone in the empty room. She sat alone and wept, inconsolably. She let out a sustained series of short, fearful cries that reverberated off the walls of the house and out into the busy yard beyond. The sort of cries unique to a grieving mother. Then she ripped at the strips of black cloth the older women had given her to wear on her arms and on her forehead as symbols of her bereavement. She had no need of symbols; her pain would be written on her forehead for all time.

It wasn't only grief that Abenaa felt for her departed daughter, or the pangs of surviving a child who'd been robbed of the chance to know a family of her own. More than grief, Abenaa felt fear that the young girl wouldn't find repose in the afterlife. She feared that Esi would become a wandering ghost, summoned in so untimely a way to the spirit world, and without the chance to beget descendants. Without this, without heirs, how could Esi become an ancestor in death? Would she be comfortable in that death, or would she be doomed to punishment, beaten or expelled by her forbearers like someone who had failed, or worse, had offended the spirits?

But as Abenaa sat weeping in her late daughter's vacated room, she was frightened too – like the men who'd carried away her inert body – that Esi's ghost could become a nuisance to those left behind. And so she'd be careful not to neglect any of her obligations. She'd be strict in observing her daughter's burial rites, to see that Esi gained safe passage, and that her spirit settled down. But just to be certain, she'd also ensure that the path back to the house was well scrambled, and that the hole in the wall had been well shut.

Preparing the body had been the bitterest task of all. As chief mourner, it fell to Abenaa alone. She'd spent the morning bathing the corpse, slowly, gently, so as not to bruise the delicate skin or disturb the child, as if she were resting. She hadn't seen the fullness of her daughter's naked body since Esi was a young girl, and so found it unrecognizable. And she found herself embarrassed about discovering this, as if there were some immodesty in it. She sang the same few prayers to herself, over and over, chanting their soothing melodies, their reassuring verses, so as not to have to think about anything else. Not to think about the grim scene in front of her. Not to think at all. She knew her duty as well as she knew her prayers: to lay out the body, prepare it for burial, and to assemble the items that would accompany her to the afterlife.

She dressed her daughter in a long white cotton robe. It was a new robe she'd worn but once, but in which her mother remembered her as being happy. She placed next to Esi the few personal items that would help her in her journey to the forever: a necklace of glass beads, a wicker-work hat, a carved wooden figurine she'd often played with as if it were a doll. She included the miniature sundial of unknown provenance the girl had loved; a secret gift from William he'd won off an English sailor, though neither had ever learned to read it. These were the only items Esi had to her name. They were trifles only, but more than might have been expected for a girl from such a modest house, and for a girl so young.

It might not have been expected either that one so young could command flag-custodians at her funeral. But there they were, at Abenaa's request, guarding the death-room, while the steady parade of friends, relatives and neighbors called at the house to laud Esi's achievements.

Esi's truncated life meant the tally of those achievements was decidedly short. So too was money for today's elaborate ceremonies. Everything had to be paid for, from those custodian guards, to a proper gift to the ancestors and to the priests. Not least, custom required the slaying of an ox, and it was this final expense that bankrupted Esi's parents. Not that there was ever a question of foregoing this crippling purchase, of buying and putting to death at least one head of cattle. Even if it meant certain ruin, no one would deny that blood today needed to be shed to prevent more adversity falling on this family. But Abenaa was equally determined that, if she and her husband were truly to be decimated by this expense, then at least none of the purchase should go to waste. So she arranged to have the hide of the animal cropped, cleaned and treated to serve as a shroud for Esi, to keep her warm in the hereafter. She made sure too that the slain beast was recovered and prepared as food for the mourners who had come to pay their respects.

And the mourners were numerous. From the dark room where she sat motionless, and when for a time her own painful wailing ceased as it pushed her beyond the point of exhaustion, Abenaa couldn't ignore the boisterous sounds of the assembly outside. Many seemed to look on aspects of the day as more festive than somber. They seemed not to be lamenting, but to be rejoicing. They were singing and dancing in noisy entertainment, celebrating the young girl's entrance into a better world, without pain or hunger or heartbreak. But Abenaa couldn't see it that way. At least, not yet she couldn't. There was nothing in this for her to celebrate. There was no comfort that her only child was closer to the cosmos, that she'd gained a more intimate relationship with all of creation. Her own relationship with her daughter had ended, cut short in a too-swift moment of imprudence. And of madness.

* *

Kwame didn't go the funeral. Not that he would have been permitted to attend, since children and unmarried adults were barred. At the mature age of nineteen he could hardly be considered a child, but as he had not yet found or been given a wife, he was certain not to be admitted all the same.

In the event, he had other plans: to find and to liberate the long-neglected canoe he and William had built over days of backbreaking effort. He would row with all his force to the heavenly shores of the secluded refuge of Bogi Cove. The cove was the ideal spot – really the only spot – he could think of. Not only because it was the one place he had always been happiest, but because that very isolation would allow him to hide how grief-stricken he was. A grown man now, he couldn't let anyone see his tears, for tears were unseemly and they were childish. And they would betray what he thought of as the greatest of faults: his weakness. He cried not only for the tragedy that was Esi's dreadful demise; he cried for his own deplorable failings.

But even that seemingly simple idea of flight didn't go to plan. The single-hulled canoe hadn't been taken out for ages, cast aside like the hooves of a sheep once its fleece was shorn and its meat consumed. The narrow boat hadn't been sheltered properly as the boys had been shown – off the ground and under a shady canopy – and it had suffered accordingly. When he found it, he saw at once that clotted grasses had grown around it, and that the moisture held in those grasses had seeped through to the teak, rotting away its underbelly like an ulcer. The decayed wood took on an unnatural color, with dark, sickly patches, and in places it crumbled into powder at his touch. The shrinking wood had placed great pressure on the joints of the canoe, and had forced sections of it to break up into blocks. A kind of porous fungus seemed to be digesting the wood itself, sprouting patches of a white, downy mass like unspun cotton, and in what Kwame at first mistook for mushrooms, though with a foul fringe and a musty odor that was more unpleasant than any mushroom he'd ever seen.

Worst of all, he couldn't manage to move the derelict canoe, to drag it on his own down to the sea, even if it had still been sea-worthy. He'd forgotten that it took two men to pull the long craft through the marshy sands. He'd never attempted to do this alone. He'd never needed to, for he'd always had William to help. It was an admission that only left him doubly frustrated, and with a palpable sense of impotence, even foolishness.

In a sudden, choleric fit, Kwame began to hack the boat to pieces. First he used the small serrated knife he kept on his belt, stabbing the rotted wood in a thousand hateful gashes as if he were stabbing a rabid wild dog. But still the beast was too big and still it threatened him, growled at him. So he assailed it with the full force of his body, kicking it with his legs, grabbing at the teetering ribs with his bare hands and throwing the mutilated pieces clear away. Some of those orphaned scraps were immediately ingested by the rapacious dunes. Other, larger chunks he eventually did manage to drag to the sea, the Infinite Sea of which

William had once crowned him king, but against which
he'd never felt anything but powerless. He surrendered the
last remnants of their once-beloved canoe to that sea, and
watched as the undercurrent carried them away, lingering
on top of the waves in plain sight, as if to taunt him. He
wished only that the pieces might quickly sink from his
view, and that he might be carried away on those currents
as well.

Alone on the beach, Kwame was hemmed in, caught
between the turbulent sea in front of him and the crush
of the funeral column not far behind. All he could bring
himself to do was to drop to his knees. All he hoped to do
was to beseech the gods, for meaning, for clemency. The
same familiar gods of whom he wavered between fearing
and loathing, whose power he both dreaded and, increasingly, he deplored. The very gods who never answered any
of his questions, let alone his prayers.

He shouted his petition loudly, so as not to be drowned
out by the rough surf and whipping wind that caused such
great noise on the beach. He entreated the ancestors to
explain why they so often withheld their grace – keeping
the fields parched, laying their people low with sickness or
hunger, despite their pleas – without any explanation, without any motive they could see. He needn't have shouted;
the gods could hear. They could cut through any noise like
fire through a spider's web. Though they were invisible,
though they refused to come out of their hiding places, he
knew they were listening.

He knew, too, that they were powerful. That they could
order the seasons to change, decide the course of rivers,
and that they alone had created this blessed place. He felt
that power in the very ground beneath him, the sands the
gods had fashioned burning the soles of his feet, the seeds

of the pepper fruits they'd devised stinging his tongue. Even Kwame couldn't doubt that it was only because of their blessings that the tribe was rich, that they were happy and strong, which is why the people honored the gods so. It was why they made the offerings, said their invocations, just the way they'd all been taught – at home, in the fields, and at the sacred grove they'd labored to keep unspoiled.

But to Kwame, the gods were selfish and they were unkind. And not only once, but again and again. And so he asked why, when he'd gone to those ceremonies in that grove, too? The rituals were so exhausting, he could barely stand at the end of them. He'd revered their name in prayers so often, he could hear them repeated over and over in his dreams. He feared them, shook at their thunderclap, and had gone hungry when they'd been displeased. But their displeasure seemed angrier with him than it ever was with the others. And so to him – although the people of the tribe were rich, happy, strong – the gods were not so kind. They were vengeful. Not generous at all. For *he* wasn't happy and *he* wasn't strong. For as long as he could remember, the spirits of his ancestors had kept a single plague knocking at his door. And it wasn't a plague of sickness or hunger they'd chosen to inflict on him, but rather the one thing he feared most: weakness.

Alone on his knees in front of them, he wasn't ashamed to admit this sin. He wasn't ashamed to accept that he'd been soft. He hadn't been the example of strength he'd wanted to be. After all, he couldn't even lift the canoe, or what was left of it. And the gods, he thought, allowed it. They wished it so. They let his father beat him, so hard and so often, until his skin glowed red like the embers of a dying bonfire. He used to think he provoked his father, that he deserved his punishment, no matter how cruel or erratic. It was part of becoming a man. He was opposing him in some way, disappointing him somehow, and so needed to be scolded. But now? Now he thought his father wasn't acting alone; he was acting as an agent of the gods, on their instructions. It wasn't that brute of a father he was disappointing, but the ancestors, whose anger his father was channeling. And in the face of such challenges, how did he fare? He fared poorly. He proved anything but the one thing he'd always wanted: to be strong.

But the terrible, spiteful gods chose only to smite him further, taking William away. Like with the cruelty of his beastly father, they allowed this to happen. They arranged to *let* William go, to have him dragged away from this place he adored, and to what fate! One he could only guess at. He shuddered to think how the chief would react if he were to learn of this treachery, or rather *when* he learned of it. He'd show them no mercy, for there wasn't any mercy in this, and there wasn't any kindness. Not at all like the compassionate gods they prayed to.

Even then, with that horrible act, even in the face of such risks to Kwame's faith, they didn't let up. No, instead they brought only greater tests. Instead, they entangled him in the death of William's love, Esi, taking her so cruelly from this world and right in front of him, setting her adrift like a cursed fisherman who can't ever find the shore.

He knew that the chief, his people, could never forgive this last offense. He couldn't, anyway, for what could be the gods' purpose in such a series of insults? To punish William? To punish him? Surely he wasn't important enough. He was insignificant, like an ant squirming around in the dried-out earth, as unimportant as the dust of that earth before a great wind. He was nothing. Not a priest, who might teach their virtuous ways. Not a chief, who might lead their people in righteousness. He wasn't even a husband yet, or a father. The gods couldn't have any use of him, other than to amuse themselves in some private game. They could throw him around like he and William used to throw sticks at the grazing cattle, to provoke them. But today, it was Kwame who was provoked.

It was impossible for him to understand. It was gutless. "I should swear at the gods for such mischief," he thought, "not praise them." When they carry out these horrible deeds, it was as if they were testing their people, and testing him to see if he could summon up the effort at last to stop all these earthly disasters from happening. They were prodding him to act, and it was intolerable. He remembered his mother telling him, "To get the fruit to fall, sometimes you have to rattle the tree." But if you rattle a tree too much, it's not just the fruit that falls, but the branches themselves. And how could he be anything but rattled? How could he do anything but fall?

Every night since Esi's death, when he was away from the glare of those who would judge him for it, he cursed himself even more than the others cursed him for allowing Esi to go to this fate alone. "Why didn't you send *me*?" he cried. It should have been him who confronted those soldiers. It should have been him who fell from the great height of that balcony. It should have been him they called on to sacrifice.

So he implored the gods to say how he'd wronged them. Was it because he once dared to want to leave this happy land they'd created? Couldn't he be forgiven that? That couldn't be thought of as such a serious offence. Many had wished the same. It was in the nature of things itself, the nature the spirits created and that they commanded – to imagine, to wonder. It was the only thing that separated the people from the beasts in the forest. His only sin was wondering whether this great world had other, better places in it, places where a man like him could be free to escape the tyranny of a ruthless father, and where he could seek meaning, even pleasure. He wondered where the crime was in that.

Still, he didn't expect the gods to console him. What he asked was that they have pity on him. He had only this one heart, and it too was weak. It was breaking, if it hadn't already broken in two. Maybe it wasn't the place of the living to ask things of the dead, especially one who hadn't proven, or yet proven, that he deserved their favor. But that's *all* he asked – to let him prove he deserved their mercy and to let him convince them of his loyalty. What he asked for was simple: he wanted them to give him strength. He wanted the strength to change things, to make things right, and to show himself worthy in their eyes, for no purpose could be served in keeping him down for so long, and for rattling him so. He'd been straining to hear their message, trying to understand it. He was listening still. He'd sworn at them, called them cowards. He'd often thought of leaving this place. But that wasn't what was in his heart and they knew it, they could see it, those who saw everything. So he asked them what sacrifice he'd have to make to demonstrate his faith. Should he slaughter an ox? He'd slaughter a team of them. Should he beat his bare shoulders with the thorniest branches of the acacia tree? He'd do this a hundred times over, until he bled or fainted from effort and exhaustion and pain. Should he kneel every day on this sultry beach, until the darkness came, until he became someone else?

He might be down now, he might seem helpless, but Kwame was sure there was strength buried deep in him yet. He'd learned this from William in their foot-races: always to keep something back, always in reserve. Now he was running a much bigger race, and though he might be worn out with grief, the race wasn't finished yet. He'd need more reserves, sure, but he was certain they were within him. He asked the spirits to help extricate them, to use them in their own service. If they were to bring William home, if the merciful gods let him have a part in achieving that *one* thing, he'd make the sacrifices they required. He'd be a vehicle not for their vengeance, but for their glory. Whatever they asked of him, he'd stand in their judgment and bow to their will, though he knew they'd give him no quarter. They never had. But this much he pledged to them.

Kwame paused to wipe the tears burning down his face, tears that were hotter than the sands beneath his feet. But in that pause, that hesitation, the gods remained silent. The earth didn't open, there was no thunder. There was only silence, except for the sounds of the rippling surf, growing louder now that the evening tides had started to roll in.

\* \*

The chief's fury hung over the household like a choking fog. It wasn't long in coming, but erupted fiercely, like a blast from a cannon, leaving a trail of vitriol in its wake like the pulverized powder the iron cannonball leaves behind. No one would have dared trying to stop him from showing his anger, from plodding around the courtyard with his walking stick cocked high as if it were divining things to destroy. And in that, he didn't lack for choices. He used the whittled stick to annihilate a collection of ceramic pots. He punctured the small barrel of imported sugar that had sat waiting to be taken to the kitchens, spilling its candied contents in every direction. Then he placed the stick itself over his bended knee and broke the rod in two, sending splintered fragments sailing across the courtyard, catching in the cloth of his robe. He wiped the splinters away while the assembled sat silent, startled and terrified. Seated at last on his wood-cut stool, he loudly banged the tobacco out of his pipe. Once. Twice. Three times, like a judge gaveling his sentence from the bench, for in fact, he was preparing to do just that: to pronounce a sentence on Kwame, whom he had summoned before him. At least, he was making this exaggerated display partly for the young man's benefit, to underscore his sense of injury, and to give emphasis to his authority, though Kwame hardly needed convincing of either.

"You dared to see the English, to enter their fort, without my permission?" roared the chief. "Men have been beaten for much less. I have swung the whip *myself* for far less, and I've enjoyed it, I tell you. You will be punished with forty lashes at least, maybe more. That's what these people would expect. That's what they want. And it's what such an outrageous violation deserves. Were it a different day, I might have expelled you, cast you out into the wilderness, for all I care. But I *will* teach you a lesson. I will teach *all* of you a lesson you'd best remember. The English are mine to manage. They are mine alone. They are not friends; they are our enemy. Our *mortal* enemy. I will not accept others bidding to our enemies, without my counsel, and without my consent. I'm not some feeble leader you can just ignore when you choose to or when it suits you. Did you think you could evade me? That your wisdom was greater than mine?"

"I thought . . ." mumbled Kwame, recoiling from fear and from shame.

"Do you have something to say? Go ahead!"

"I thought . . . I only wanted to help, that's all. I thought I could help."

"Is that so?" said the chief. "And look at what your help has wrought. Tragedy. Humiliation. You've humiliated our people, that poor girl's family, and you have humiliated me. What other kind of *help* are you offering? What other liberties did you think you could take? Do you wish to issue my orders? Do you want to sit on my stool, in my place? Yes, come. Come sit here. Take my place. I'll sit on the floor with the others, shall I? On the dusty floor, soiling my robe, like my wives, my children, my subjects."

"Oh Eno," chimed in Eukobah. "Be gentle on the boy. He's as distraught as you are angry. Even you can see, the boy meant no harm."

"Be gentle? On the boy? The *boy* is a man in his prime and old enough to think for himself. He's old enough to know the rules, and to bear the consequences of his actions. To bear the consequences of defying me, his chief. Who among you doesn't know the rules? Discipline. Obedience. This is all I ask of my people. And in return, I bring you justice. I bring you peace. Without discipline, I am nothing. *We* are nothing. It cannot be tolerated."

"My only intention . . ." struggled Kwame again, as feebly as the last attempt.

"Silence," said the chief. "I won't permit any more of this. I will not be interrupted, and I will not be defied. You'll be punished, be certain of that."

"Eno," whispered Eukobah into her husband's ear. "He was trying to help. To help not just that poor girl, but to help get back our son. Your son. Your son who's been kept from us by these vile English for far too long. Enough is enough, Eno, he must be brought home. It's been more than three years, without so much as a word from him. If there's anything that can't be tolerated here, then it must be this. It's a slander, such disrespect to you, to your pride, is it not? How can we blame him for doing what any one of us might have done, and should have done ourselves? I had half a mind to do the same, to march right up to those high walls and confront that governor myself. And if you must know, Eno, I encouraged the girl."

"What do you mean, you encouraged her? How?"

"Yes, that's right, she set off to the fort with my knowledge, and with my help; with the help of *all* the women here in fact. She asked us for guidance, and we gave it to her. We allowed it to happen. If anyone here is to be punished, then it ought to be us." She knew this was something her husband could never bring himself to do.

"Be quiet, wife, let me think. My mind is too clouded with rage."

"Be still, husband, be calm," she sighed, placing a hand gently on his head. "Your anger is like a poison: it inflames you, it blurs your judgment, and it's your clear judgment that keeps all of us safe," she continued, flattering his pride in a way she knew he couldn't possibly resist. She knew he'd swallow such compliments like he swallowed good drink, that he'd find it sweet regardless of how much of it he swilled.

The chief paused. He stared coldly ahead for a long while, while the others sat around him in silence, afraid they might catch his eye and provoke his anger.

"Yes, we've certainly put up with enough. We can't allow this insult any longer. And you," he said, turning to Kwame, still crouching before him, "you will make it right. Your punishment will wait for another day. In the meantime, you'll go again to see the governor."

"Eno!" shrieked Eukobah.

"Go again? To the fort?" cried Kwame, bewildered by this perfidious order. "But they will butcher me!"

"They'll do no such thing. Yes, you will go again. You will demand the return of my son, William. But this time, you'll do so from a position of strength. This time, you'll do so with my might behind you. You will take a company of men the likes of which those spineless intruders have never seen before. You will march right up to that fat, faint-hearted man who calls himself a governor and show him that no Englishman can mistreat my people. Tell him, we are the masters here, not him, and he should never forget it. Take my message that William, our son, will be returned to us, or else it is England that will pay, and pay dearly. Slowly, I'll strangle them until they yield," declared the chief. "Tell him this. Be certain he understands," he said, as he signaled with an imperious wave for Kwame to quit his presence.

And so Kwame took his leave. But as he crossed the same patch of yard in front of the compound where Esi had camped out for a week's time, Eukobah quickly caught up with him. It was the first opportunity she'd had to speak to him since Esi's death.

"Kwame," she said, "I know you to be William's dear friend and I know you to be true, to be honorable. So, do as the chief says. As he instructs you to do. But trust me, there's hope in this. There's a chance in it, though it may not seem like it to you yet. A chance to get our William home, and a chance for you to redeem yourself in the chief's eyes."

"Do you really think so?"

"Of course I do. And Kwame, don't be afraid. I know it seems like a dark day. But remember, son: that however dark the sky, there will always be a morning. If you remember this, repeat this – even as you go toward danger, even when the threat seems greatest – know that you'll be safe in the protection of the ancestors. That is their promise to those who really *are* true and honorable. And that is my promise to you."

"However dark the sky," echoed Kwame, "there will always be a morning. Yes, I will try to remember. I'll try to be true. And if the gods wish it, I believe – I know – I will be safe."

Eukobah took his hands in hers, and together they prayed. Together they set about to chase away the malice and the disdain with which Kwame had only too recently cursed the spirits. Those same spirits whose safety and shelter, never more than today, he would now require.

\* \*

Kwame's arrival at the fort that morning could hardly have contrasted more dramatically with that of his previous visit. Unlike his last attempt, he didn't need to plead his case to the guards, to petition them for entry; he didn't need to offer a bribe of gold, or an inducement of any kind. He arrived not alone, but at the front of a force more convincing than any bribe, more persuasive than any cutting or cunning words he could think of. He carried high the chief's yellow and black ensign, while the column of men behind him stretched long, every one of them banging his drum as loud as a rousing north wind, as if he were beating the charge of the cavalry. The English soldiers knew well the sounds of those drums, announcing the visit of the chief or of his representative. Yet this morning, the music of the drums was somehow different, swifter, more jarring. It carried with it more foreboding than usual. And as the music changes, so does the dance. This time, the dance was more than just posturing. This time there was real, patent menace in the advancing movement of the men. Today the English would not just be impressed by this formation; they would be shaken by it and they would be cowed. Everything had been designed to ensure it would be so.

Kwame marched anxiously at the head of this large contingent, dressed in elaborate finery, as if he were going into battle. As if he were royalty. The flowing garment of *nmewntoma* cloth he wore instantly lent him an air of great dignity. It was the kind of robe usually reserved for important occasions, military and religious alike, and for men of some nobility, of some position. It had been draped over his right shoulder in generous plaits, but still hugged closely at his waist and kept his athletic arms exposed. It was made of the same finely woven cloth of silk and cotton, the same bold geometric pattern, as the long-sleeved tunic William's sisters had stitched for him to take on his journey to London, and that Captain Crichton had quickly stripped off his passenger with savage violence, tossing it unceremoniously off the side of the *Lady Carolina* into the sea. And although the weave and the fabric were the same, the robe Kwame wore didn't share the same colors of indigo blue and yellow that had graced William's tunic, but rather was dominated by varying shades of red, the symbols of blood and sacrifice and struggle. For there would surely be struggle ahead.

Still extremely nervous, he'd wear the imposing robe as if it were a costume in a drama, and he looked on the courtyard of the fort as if it were a stage set. He'd play his leading part in this production with aplomb: he'd deliver his lines with a confidence and a fluency that was absent off-stage. It wouldn't be the flinching, diffident Kwame who appeared;

that wasn't what the part called for. He'd be a fearless actor, rendering this speech, this impeachment, with the authority of someone who'd been mediating disputes – or at least play-acting so – for years, though he'd never been in anything like this position before. He'd never once exercised supremacy over anyone, let alone such a potent figure as the governor. His self-assured, almost insolent delivery and the emphatic nature of the lines he improvised, would startle everyone. His deadpan performance might even have been applauded by the other men, if the setting hadn't been so deadly grave.

None would have been prouder than William to see his friend take on this assumed role, to pronounce these invented lines with such fortitude and to see him dressed this way. They might, however, have laughed at the sound made by the plentiful beads he wore, clanging together in loud discord with every step Kwame took. There were beads on the headband, on the heavy necklace, armbands and bracelets of gold, just as there were on the spear and flag pole he carried. These adornments proved almost too great a burden for his well-developed but still slim frame to bear and, though meant only to enhance his prestige, might well have seemed comical.

But today there would be no place for laughter. Today he would need to bear any burden. He wore these ornaments, he inhabited them, like the honor they were intended to be, and as an instrument of the power they were meant to convey. Any hesitation he had was buried under the weight of this lofty costume – worn with the same pride as might any respected member of the community, as he hoped he'd at last become. He was without question being treated as one. It lulled him into forgetting that he only wore this exquisite robe and jewelry as a manifestation of the chief's punishment, that he should confront again the bullheaded English forces in the chief's name.

Had there been a mirror in which to see his reflection, Kwame wouldn't have recognized himself. Certainly Governor Marsh, who emerged from the main house to meet the arriving forces, didn't recognize him as the visitor who just a few days ago he'd referred to insolently as a "patsy" and who, spying him in the courtyard waiting apprehensively with Esi, he'd dismissed out of hand. He wouldn't see him as a patsy today.

"The chief has given me clear instructions," Kwame told the twitchy governor. "He's directed me to tell his people here, these men and women you employ for such cheap wages, to lay down their tools and to put aside whatever task they're doing. They are to stop their work altogether. He wants to make it very clear to you and your men, that from this moment on we will slowly drain the life from this place. We will chip away at your arrogance and your pride, until you return to us, to the chief, what is most valuable to him."

"And what might that be?" asked the governor, with an undisguised and unrepentant note of bombast in his voice.

"His son William, of course. The son he left in your care, that he entrusted to you to send to your dear England. To keep him away for so long, well we can only guess at why. His studies there must be complete, his business there fulfilled. We can only speculate what use you might have for him anymore, and none of the answers we can think of is satisfactory. He must be returned, and it must be soon."

"This isn't within my power," said Governor Marsh. "I know of the chief's son, of course. I vaguely recall having met him once or twice while the chief and I were discussing the terms of his mission to England. But I can't demand his return, it isn't within my prerogative to do so. Besides, I can't even be certain to know where he is."

"Then you must find out, and you must return him safe to Annamaboe. To his father, who I tell you, will not stand for anything less," shot back Kwame, at this point more than just limping his way through this play-acting, but by now thoroughly enjoying it. So much so that he felt emboldened to raise ever higher the tone of his attempted intimidation. "This isn't a request, or some sort of negotiation. This is an order from the chief. Send whatever messages you need to back to your masters in England. Ask the traders or the ships' captain to help, but it's for you to find him. All I can ensure you in the meantime, all *we* can ensure you," he said, pointing markedly to the many similarly outfitted men who surrounded him, "is that you will be motivated to do so. We will persuade you, if you still need persuading. Until you do, I can guarantee you only one thing: that you will bear the consequences," he said, drawing on precisely the same construction the chief had earlier used, in his own language, in passing sentence on Kwame.

"Bear the consequences?" said Governor Marsh. "Whatever can you mean by *that*?"

"Just as I said. These men and women are to stop their work. When I leave here, most will leave with me. We won't stop doing so many things at once that you starve. No, we're more charitable than that. Today we stop doing your washing and plucking the feathers from your rotting chickens. From tomorrow, you'll have to risk the forests for yourselves, to find and chop the firewood you need. Soon you'll need to start hauling the water for yourselves up this great hill. We won't starve you, not yet, but we will withdraw enough so that we're certain, so that the chief is certain, it hurts. That you suffer and that the suffering gets more painful all the time."

"Am I to believe my ears? Do you threaten an English officer? Have you any idea, any idea at all, of the risk you are taking? The power we have? What you really are up against?"

"Power?" replied Kwame, more cocksure than ever. "You are nothing! Your so-called power, your weapons, will be nothing when your stomachs are empty, when you wheeze from thirst and shiver from the cold in the night. Every month we'll come here – *I'll* come here – to withdraw something else, some other service, until you're left begging like dogs and come crawling on your knees to the chief to beg his forgiveness. And that is something, I can tell you, he's not currently in a state of mind to provide."

"And if we fail? What if this William eludes us, and cannot be found in our realm? What if he doesn't *want* to return here?"

"Nonsense, he'll want to return. And if you don't see to this, if William doesn't walk freely down the plank of one of your great ships before six months are out, well then we'll hit you where it'll hurt you most."

"Meaning?"

"Meaning, we'll cut off not just your supplies and our labor, we will cut off our trade. Not a single new slave will be delivered to you. The vaults here will be emptied. Just as the gold you've stolen from us over the years has dried up, so too will our supply of captives."

This was the cruelest blow of all, and the one the governor feared most. It was also the one on which his standing, his career, could too easily be forfeited. To lose a shipment of the king's cargo at sea, or preside over a spiraling budget of upkeep for the outpost, might be regrettable. Even to see the territory's gold supply peter out was lamentable, but it could be foreseen by the mandarins in London, and it could be managed. But to cause the flow of slaves to be interrupted, perhaps even to lose control of the concession itself, this would be a damnable, grievous offense. And they both knew it.

"You've heard the deadline," continued Kwame. "The chief won't tolerate this situation continuing without end. You have just six months from today. No more than that. I'm to come here at every full moon, without fail, to check on the progress you've made, to relay any news you have of William to the chief. And to impose the stricter punishments he wishes, until you deliver what he's requested. And with the gods to protect us, with the gods as my witnesses, you *will* deliver."

Without a word further, Kwame turned and withdrew. He left the governor's presence with considerably more flare and bravado than when he'd entered the site. And as he left the fort, with a line of workers in tow, he was a changed man. Evoking the testimony and the protection of the same gods he just days before had cursed for their truculence, he was transformed. He stood taller, took longer strides, looked straight ahead when he walked and not sheepishly down at the patchy red earth. He was a man who might have been forgiven for thinking that he'd finally captured the ear of those elusive gods, and that his desperate pleas for strength, appeals that only a short while ago had brought him to his knees, were at last being answered.

As he and the other men returned to the chief's compound – their mission successfully discharged and their report of it made – Badu, the eldest son of their ruler, was not among their number. He hadn't taken part in the expedition to the English citadel, a campaign he might otherwise have been expected to lead. He was still many miles away to the west, carrying out with diligence the other, more underhanded part of his father's instructions: to court the covetous detachment of French soldiers and private French traders, who were as eager as a bridegroom to consummate a new alliance and to exploit the chief's growing impatience and irritation with their enemy of old, the English, from which they could only stand to profit.

Badu rested comfortably within the well-furnished French encampment, seated on cushions of silk and velvet, treated to generous amounts of the brandies about which his education in Paris had made him a self-declared expert. He bumbled happily through the half-dozen or so phrases of their language he half-remembered, all with a joyful if notional sense of nostalgia. But the haze of that nostalgia, and the warm intoxication of the drink, blotted out the hard reality of his time in Paris, a period marked by frequent blasts of biting, wintry cold and too many sunless days. There had been the discomfort of so much that was new and unfamiliar, and above all, the raw loneliness that had defined it.

It was the same aching loneliness that another young Fante man was enduring half a world away, toiling without reprieve on a sugar plantation under the blinding Barbados sun. William had lived every day in that hostile land smarting from almost unbearable pangs of solitude and heartache, convinced he had been forgotten. Abandoned. He'd been given a new name, a new identity, but still he doggedly kept alive his dreams of home. He nurtured dreams of his mother and sisters, of his carefree excursions with Kwame, and of Esi most of all. Esi, about whose contemptible fate he was completely ignorant. He was ignorant, too, that the great might of the English Crown was soon to be mobilized with a single objective in mind. To find him. And to release him.

## • CHAPTER 13 •

It had taken Gareth Bain several weeks to get used to his new spectacles. Unlike his old pair, they weren't made of heavy steel and coin silver, but of a lightweight, marble-grey horn. The lenses were larger, and perfectly round, in a way that drew attention to the high cheekbones on his face. A gracious face that, even before he slipped on his striking new glasses, had always invited examination. Contrary to his previous pair, this apparatus didn't rest flatly on his sharp-edged nose, but had an arched bridge to anchor it well in place. It featured spring-loaded side arms that pushed up against his temples, then disappeared entirely behind his high-set ears, and copper hinges that allowed the whole thing to fold, effortlessly, like an accordion.

But he'd soon found that those arms pressed too hard, and the pinching sensation caused him to suffer debilitating headaches. These were only magnified by the trouble he had in adjusting to the step-change in correction, and by his false assertion that the improved lenses were aggravating the motion sickness he was suffering on board the ship. For it wasn't the spectacles that were causing his unease, but the relentless convulsing of the craft, coupled with the lack of ventilation in his well-furnished but very small cabin. He was experiencing the worst of the dizziness

and nausea about which he'd been warned by helpful col-
leagues in London, who'd offered him exhortations about
the arduous journey they'd done before him, and that he'd
so easily, and so regrettably, dismissed.

The horn frames, however, had begun to slacken over
the three-month journey, and now sat much more comfortably. Still, the more comfortable they turned out to be, the
more nervous about them Gareth became, for he only had
this one pair, and he'd paid more than he should have, and
easily more than he could afford. The expense accounted
for almost two weeks of his wages as a mid-level clerk in
the Royal African Company. They were wages that would
arguably have been better spent on settling persistent ar-
rears with his tight-fisted landlord, or with a host of others
who laid claim to the growing litany of his casual debts.

And so he'd taken to handling the spectacles gingerly,
as prized as if they were faceted gems. When not on his
head, he took care to wrap them delicately in their rawhide
case, whose interior was itself costly, lined as it was with
expensive red japanning.

He was holding them guardedly in his hands when the
two men arrived at the door of his cabin. The two burly
men, whose skin was as black as dry gunpowder, were
dressed like lowly farmhands, barefoot and in tatty cotton clothes that reeked of wood-smoke. Taking them for
slaves, he let out a kind of strangled squeal, dropping the
spectacles on the floor, which created a wholly new terror,
that the horn might have cracked in the fall.

It was an inauspicious start to his arrival in Annamaboe. The men were not captives; they were lackeys sent
this morning to meet the newly moored ship, and in particular to help the clerk disembark. They were two of the
dwindling number of Fante still employed by the English,

months after the chief began to withdraw all but the most basic services, and to divert his attentions to the French. The chief was following through on his promise. He was making good on his threat.

It was hardly surprising that Gareth should be hostile to the appearance of these men; everything in this strange land would seem hostile to him. After all, he'd never been to West Africa. Indeed, he'd never been more than a jerky carriage ride away from his central city flat, except for the hurried visits to the seaside towns on the Sussex coast, to which he'd enjoyed taking a string of devoted lady friends. More surprising still, in all the time he'd been in the employ of the civil service, he'd hardly ever managed to interact directly with the free African men that were ubiquitous within it. Men who, in the teeming offices of the Company where he worked, performed most of the menial domestic duties. Day and night they filled the inkwells, brought up tea from the basement kitchens, straightened the meeting rooms after disorderly, late-night sessions, and scrubbed clean the water closets – lurking always in the massive building's spectral shadows. He'd been taught to think of these men only as clouded forms, as faceless servants, not out of a lack of kindness, but out of a lack of proper consideration. Mostly he'd come to know the men of Africa simply as the Company's principal commodity. They were entries in a ledger-book of the flourishing slave trade: where they came from, whether they'd been processed in London, Bristol or in Liverpool, and where they were to be sent. They weren't people whose names, stories, lives were to be valued.

In truth, the men pulling together the affairs in the clerk's cabin were as uninterested in their charge as he was in them. They attended to the mess they found there, all the while contending with the skittish looks he tried – in vain – to fight from throwing them, especially when packing his more personal effects. To the chief's men, it hardly seemed worth the paltry wage they were being paid. The only pleasure they took in it was in making sure the wary Englishman was genuinely distressed in their presence, moving in so stiflingly close to him, he could taste the burnt betel nut on their breath.

Fortunately the ship's British crew was quick to his rescue. The sailors had warmed to him on the long voyage, despite finding him at first to be impossibly foppish. He was the archetype of the well-meaning but wide-eyed bureaucrat they'd too often been burdened with ferrying around the globe, but he'd shown himself to be full of good humor, and often laughed as loudly as they did at their jokes, including those at his expense. For weeks, his often preposterous requests had amused them no end, ranging from the trivial to the irrational. He complained he couldn't sleep, despite being afforded the finest cabin on the starboard side, and asked ever-so-politely if the captain couldn't possibly make the boat pitch less. When they couldn't meet his requests for more varied foods and more varied reading material – as if these things could effortlessly be conjured up – they mercilessly ribbed him because of it. They'd asked, for instance, whether he'd prefer the laundry to prepare his undergarments with or without starch, if he favored the speckles on his quail eggs to be olive or brown in color, and what diameter of rain pellet would be most to his liking. To their astonishment, he quickly came to find this derisive heckling humorous, which only encouraged them more.

His shipmates had in fact long since worked out that he'd confused the ship for what was likely his second-tier gentleman's club in the West End, since they surmised –

196 * ROBERT GLICK

correctly – he wouldn't have the stature or the connections to get into White's or the Beefsteak Club or any of the other, more aristocratic establishments in St. James's. They suspected, too, that the waiters and the assistants at his club would have been just as entertained as they were with his comical, sometimes scurrilous talk. He had endless trivia about lesser-known historical events, gossip about ill-behaved nobles and political intrigue at Court, and unreliable predictions about the outcome of bad-tempered disputes in the colonies. These were things about which the ship's otherwise hard-boiled crew could hardly get enough.

But they were also concerned for him, for they knew Gareth would find it hard to grapple with the conditions in Africa. Even the lance corporal waiting for him this morning on the quay could immediately see that this demure dandy would have a hard time of it. He'd struggle here in Annamaboe, and then in Barbados, where he and the crew would be headed in only a few days' time. It was hard to imagine anyone being more out of place on the uncompromising Gold Coast. Gareth's fanciful spectacles were simply the opener. His clothes, for one thing, were entirely wrong. The close-fitting silk waistcoat, with its brass buttons and its narrow-fitting cuffed sleeves, made him as flashy as the governor in full dress uniform. His square-toed shoes had small, oblong buckles that might have been right for a glittery house party, but would be ludicrous in this terrain. He had three identical pairs of them, the tongue rising so high above his ankle they seemed better suited as a jackboot for riding or for a footman serving cocktails. He lacked only for braided garters and a bob wig to make him seem more hapless.

His constitution seemed as ill-fitted for the circumstances as his wardrobe, and as he stepped out of his cabin and into the blistering sunlight he looked as if the voyage – the oppressive heat, the uninterrupted hazards at sea – had taken everything out of him. His handsome features were drawn, and there was barely any color left in his cheeks as he shuffled down the gang-plank and onto the shore. As Gareth bent down to grab his knees, for a moment the corporal thought he might be intending to kiss the solid ground, the first he'd been on since they'd touched down briefly in the north of Portugal, and that was already many weeks ago. There he'd happily procured several bottles of fortified wine with which to fortify himself, generously sharing his windfall with the senior crew; but these had long since dried up, and he'd had little with which to steady himself since. But he wasn't bending down to embrace the earth; he did so because he was light-headed, and was trying to fill his lungs with air. In any event, he wouldn't have dared to touch the ground with his lips, terrified as he was to fall sick and paranoid that disease and affliction might lie around every corner. He'd be as ill at ease in this alien land as a sinner at Sunday prayers.

But though unhinged by the journey, he'd bounce back soon enough. It was nothing that a hot bath, freshly laundered clothes and a well-seasoned meal couldn't make right. A meal that, if his prayers were answered, would include an ample choice of the fresh fruits and vegetables the ship's kitchen so desperately lacked. With that, his health and his mood would steadily be restored. It was the same simple, effective formula that had been applied to the long line of wearied visitors – of auditors, chroniclers, curates and clerks – who'd come before him.

Governor Marsh waited patiently for him at the fort, ready to apply these remedies as he'd so often done previously, and no doubt would be called on soon to do again.

He'd done so for men much haughtier than this one, zeal-
ous men who arrived to inspect the site, to advise, to record
the goings-on in scrupulous detail, and when it came to
it, never quite managed to figure out how things actually
worked on the ground. They were men the governor knew
to be educated at the finest universities – who studied the
area and its commerce for years, pored over intricately coded maps in the offices of the Board of Trade and Plantations, who prepared meticulous reports for the government
of the day – and who invariably seemed to leave the Gold
Coast understanding less about the place than when they
first arrived. The governor wasn't narrow-minded or naïve,
but his experience with the likes of Gareth Bain had led
him to believe that, although not all dimwits were clerks,
all clerks were dimwitted.

The governor and Abigail had prepared for his arrival
with the minimal service required. They'd aired out the
unremarkable bedroom down the hall from their own, took
care to tie up the Norfolk spaniel in the gunnery hall so
its bark wouldn't disturb the new arrival, and set a table
with the copious meal they knew he'd be spoiling for. And
after the long walk up from the quay, as Gareth eventually
entered the house, the governor stood in the entryway to
receive him, offering a hyperbolic salute that was as unnecessary as it was unwarranted for one not of military rank,
but which Governor Marsh thought his visitor might consider his due.

Gareth was grateful for such a warm welcome. He was
doubly pleased to be received in the dining room by Abigail, dressed as colorfully as a maypole, with a long per-
iwinkle-blue silk ribbon in her hair and a small, sparkly
jewel around her slender neck – the one valuable bauble
she'd been brave enough, or ill-advised enough, to bring

from Gloucestershire. She more than caught his eye, so un-expected was her grace and beauty in such a forlorn place.

They sat down to lunch almost immediately. Even the tableware she'd laid out for the meal suggested a kind of deliverance to him, for her fine china with its enchanting butterfly motif made for a far more appetizing prospect than the grubby wooden bowls he'd never quite gotten used to on the journey here. While the governor seemed preoccupied – cutting the cigar he'd smoke once the short meal finished, indecorously picking out the stubborn flakes of mud lodged under his thumbnail with the tine of a fork – Abigail issued pointed instructions to the cook that were at best only half-followed.

At the small round table, Abigail sat herself so close to the clerk, several times she brushed his shoulder as she carefully poured out the soup. She was so close he could drink in the lavender perfume on the ribbon in her hair. The smell of a woman was usually as familiar to him as a popular music-hall tune, but lately the measure of its rhyme had started to slip from his memory. But here, in Abigail's presence, he felt giddy as his memory returned. He felt emboldened to join almost immediately into the animated conversation she had begun, prattle the governor considered so inane that it infuriated him, anxious as he was to enter into more substantive discussions. But in this, he'd have to wait.

"Did they rid us of that cad?" she asked. "Did they hang the Jacobite traitor after all?"

"Who's that, Abi?" asked the governor.

"I assume you mean Lovat? The Lord Simon Lovat?" replied Gareth, with a knowing smile.

"The very one," she said.

"I see you're well informed, my lady," he continued,

flattering her as if she were a titled member of some privileged class, as was her one ambition.

"My wife, she reads all the journals," said the governor. "Backwards and forwards. *The Examiner*, *The Daily Courant*, *The Spectator*. Whatever she can get her hands on. Though out here, of course, the news is somewhat delayed, when it comes at all."

"Out here, the news is irrelevant," she retorted. "Anyway, that man, that traitor, he's a villain, Thomas. He kidnapped that poor Lady Amelia to make her his wife and to get his greedy hands on her lands and titles. He treated her abominably!"

"I'm sure you're right, dear."

"And what's more," she added, unfalteringly, "he's a Papist. He wants to see a Catholic back on the throne. Imagine such a thing. He'd see our gracious king bow again to Rome. Beheading would be too good for the likes of him. He should rot in a damp cell in his precious Highlands swamp, I say."

"My, my, what hostility, my dear," said the governor, taken aback by her fervor. "It's not as if this Lubbad . . ."

"Lovat," she corrected him.

"It's not as if this Lord *Lovat* robbed your family's tombs!"

"He might just as well have done."

"Well," interjected Gareth, "they cut off his head all the same. With an axe on Tower Hill."

"Well thank the Lord almighty for that."

"It's only that . . . well, it didn't exactly go as the executioner had planned. Quite the tragedy, in fact. About twenty others went with him, before the main event."

"Goodness," said Abigail, "whatever can you mean? Who were they?"

"Spectators on the grandstand, crowded onto the scaffold. They'd come to watch. To gawk. There were so many of them, the whole thing caved in, and crushed the lot of them."

"Serves them right," said the governor. "It's too macabre to want to witness an execution like that."

"The most galling bit? The incident appeared to amuse the condemned man," said Gareth. "The papers took to saying he 'laughed his head off,' if you can believe such poor taste."

"How ghastly," Abigail barely managed to say, as Gareth – by instinct – went to reach out to take her nearby arm, to console her, as he would any pretty, unnerved woman, before he remembered himself.

By now, Governor Marsh was fed up with this distraction, and signaled that his wife should excuse herself. She did so, reluctantly, and although she retired from the room, she didn't hesitate to listen at the door.

"But what news of the chief's son? What news of that William?" asked the governor, impatiently. "What does Captain Crichton have to say for himself?"

"Crichton has nothing more to say on the subject."

"Why's that?"

"Because Crichton is dead."

"*Dead*? Did one of his crew put a knife in the thug's back? It would hardly surprise me."

"No, no," said Gareth, "nothing as subversive as all that. Though if his black-hearted reputation is to be believed, I suppose that could well have been his fate one day. No, he died of scurvy, so I'm told, like too many of our sailors. And a horrible death, that is, I can tell you. I've seen for myself some of the afflicted men in hospital, robbed of their energy. Before the end, they look ruined, already like corpses. They can't lift their arms, and the fever over-takes them. It's a truly horrible sight. It's what got Crichton, according to the account I got from his ship's first mate, an earnest, well-travelled fellow called Spike who tended to the captain 'til his last day. That day came just before the crew made London. He said the captain had all the signs: spots on his face and arms, pale as parchment. This Spike, he said by the end Crichton had lost so many of his teeth and that his gums were bleeding so badly, his mouth looked like a sponge. He says the look in his eyes promised only the death that was shortly to come."

"That's certainly not the man *I* knew," said the governor. "He was the very picture of health when he last left us."

"Scurvy can bring down the most able-bodied of men. But the worst of it, for our purposes anyway if not for his, is that his men couldn't get a word out of him. There wasn't a word about William, or anything else for that matter, except to confirm what we knew already."

"Which is . . .?"

"Which is that the captain sold the boy to a market trader in Bridgetown. He fetched a hefty price at that. But from then on, the boy disappeared. He vanished into one of the hundreds of plantations out there, without a trace."

"And what of the ship? What of the *Lady Carolina*?"

"Taken out of service, I'm afraid. She got pretty badly torn about on that last trip of hers from the West Indies. What was left was sold for scrap. Her lead plates and bronze nails were melted down. Apparently there was barely enough to salvage for a statue of a deer in Hyde Park."

"And the rest of her crew?"

"Dispersed. I dare say, they'd have been glad to see the back of her. They were all risking their lives on such a dicey vessel, every time she went to sea. Toward the end, more than one quit his post rather than sail on her. And, well, I can't say I blame any of them."

"Blast," said Governor Marsh. "What a conspiracy against us! How will we ever find the boy now?"

"Well, that's the thing. We think we might have managed to find him already."

"What do you mean *might* have? Either you have or you haven't. Which is it? This isn't exactly the time for equivocation. My men will riot if we don't settle this whole damn affair in short order."

"Our forces have been scouring the islands for weeks. For months. And they report having found a boy in the Dash Valley who says he's William."

"Who *says* he is? What kind of game are you playing at, Bain?"

"Bear with me, governor. The boy has all the traits of your chief's son. He seems to answer to that name. He's known to practice all the Fante rites and to know all their prayers, but to what god they're praying, I couldn't tell you."

"Indeed. Would that they had but one god!"

"He also has the leopard tattoo, the same three straight lines and the cluster of dots we had a description of, and that I saw this very morning on the men who carried my luggage up from the ship. But then again, I'm told many of the men out there have similar markings."

"So what makes you think this one is William?"

"Because this one, above all, knows English, and he knows it well. Not many of them can say that. His owner – an influential nobleman and, apparently, as cantankerous a character as you or I are ever likely to meet – says he's invaluable because of it. It allows the boy to serve as a kind of intermediary, a peacemaker between his overseers and his slaves. He keeps the latter in line, and because of it, his owner won't discharge him or sell him. He says the boy's much too useful. But this is the really disingenuous part: at the same time he's presented His Majesty's government with a long list of demands, some bits of which would raise the king's hackles if anyone were brave enough to actually show them to him."

"What can he want?" asked the governor. "Five hundred pounds? Six hundred?"

"Oh no, it's much more than that he wants."

"So a thousand pounds? Are you to tell me we can't make this problem go away for a thousand bloody pounds?"

"Not for that amount alone, no. His demands are greater than that. They're more extensive anyway. It's not money alone he's seeking. He wants preferential trading rights for his sugar crop. He wants a commendation from His Majesty . . . and then some!"

"So go get him. Go get the boy. Steal him if you have to, send in the Royal Navy, for goodness sake, that's what it's there for."

"It isn't quite that simple, sir. The plantation owners, right across the island, right across the provinces, would take to arms if we came in by force and commandeered their rightful property like that. Besides, it's more than the money that bothers me, it's more even than the many other terms he's demanding."

"What then?" sighed the governor, visibly riled.

"I'm concerned it might not be him. That it might not be William."

"But a moment ago, you said it *was* him."

"No, I said it *might* be. This boy knows he'd be freed. They *all* know. The whole island does. Our troops have been making such a fuss about this, the boy could be bluffing.

And frankly, I needn't tell you, we can't get it wrong. If we were to waste another year getting there and bringing back, well . . . bringing back the wrong boy, we'd be made to look more than laughable. We might lose our heads over it."

"Like Lord Lovat."

"The very same. We might lose this concession. You and I would lose our posts, that's for sure."

The governor, who scrupulously prepared for every contingency as if he were going into battle, hadn't thought this particular scenario through. And so, plainly frustrated, he stood up from his chair and began to pace furiously around the paneled dining room, like a prisoner newly thrown into a narrow cell. He moved toward the sideboard, intending to replenish his empty whiskey glass, only to walk away again so distracted that the glass remained unfilled. He stared out of the large window across the vast horizon, as if he were trying to see all the way across the Atlantic to the colonies, trying to detect an answer there to this unexpected conundrum.

"Look," he said, "there must be a way to resolve this. An easy way. I'll stew on it a while. In the meantime, I'd already planned to spend this night at Fort Hamilton, a few miles down the coast, to inspect our troops there first thing tomorrow. We'll be leaving soon, to be sure to get there before nightfall. Why don't you join me? We can discuss this problem further on the way. And you'll see a little of how these godforsaken people live. It would be a little color to tell the folks back home."

"As much as I'd like to see a bit more of this place for myself, no, thank you. I don't think I could bear another journey yet. I've barely got my land-legs back, and any more tossing about might very well do me in. I'm afraid I wouldn't be very good company to you."

"Very well, then. We'll discuss it when I return. In the meantime, do try and get some rest here tonight. If they haven't done so already, I'll have someone bring your things to the room. I expect you'll want a bath to be drawn as well. I do hope, in any event, you can make the most of your stay with us. Enjoy it while you can, I'd say, as you'll be off again on that low-down ship soon enough!"

The anticipation of getting back on the waves to make the second, more precarious leg of his triangular journey did indeed fill Gareth with trepidation. But at least now he'd have an idea of what to expect on the crossing to the Americas; what he hadn't counted on was the disquiet that overcame him at the prospect of two nights in the fort's uninviting bedroom to which the couple had assigned him. Despite the admittedly minimal trouble they'd gone to in fitting it out for his stay, he knew right away he wouldn't be comfortable.

At least the room didn't careen like those on the ship, but it was hardly any less shabby than the quarters he'd just vacated. In many respects, it was worse. From the outset, he was greeted by broad cracks in the plaster around the tapered doorframe, by the unusually sparse furnishings, and by the almost complete lack of ornamentation. The only decoration was the mangy paper pasted to the walls, which in places stopped well above the skirting boards, and that on the sunny, south-facing part of the room had already begun to discolor. He thought of this paper-trim as nothing short of dishonest, made to imitate the tapestries and silk draperies that hung in more refined surroundings. He'd seen more and more of this kind of tawdry gimmickry in drawing rooms at home, printed in relief on blocks of fruitwood and infused with an increasingly common damask design. In this room, the design had been printed onto small, square sheets of paper, dipped in one of two colors – teal and charcoal, each duller than the other – and had produced a textured finish that left the damasks looking as if they were lightly raised. The consequence, especially now in the evening's low candlelight, was to make them seem three-dimensional, and eerily alive. The bold forms appeared to move with the light, an ominous effect exacerbated by the fact that the sheets had been pasted together unevenly so that they overlapped, and so that the pattern didn't line up properly. This, too, spoke to him of shoddiness and neglect.

But this was nothing compared to the room's real concern: the creatures that crept along the papered wall itself, and that clung to it like ivy climbing an oak tree. He counted at least six of the sinister vermin. The trick of the candlelight produced the same effect on them as it had on the wallpaper, elongating their shapes, making them appear to jump excitedly from place to place, to disappear and reappear as quickly as the light shifted.

He'd never seen anything remotely like the two lizards. The long-tailed salamander looked menacingly as if it had horns, as it moved across the wall with a kind of cocky, swaying gait. It was trailed by a spotted gecko that might have been prehistoric, with its long snout and scaly skin sheathed in blotches of yellow. Its tongue darted out like an arrow, startling Gareth every time. Lying completely still for long minutes, it stared back at him with piercing eyes, as if trying to communicate its indignity. And then there were the insects, whirling about his head. The moths hovering near the flame he could identify; it was the ones in the darkness that really disturbed him, especially the beetles, one of which he'd stepped on in first entering the room. He'd heard the crack of its hard skeleton. Even its wings were as hard as cobble-stone. He watched one of them walk awkwardly across the floor, perch itself on its hind legs, then sort of bounce before taking flight. Every time it did so, his heart leapt with it. And despite the fine muslin netting, he worried that his bed would be infested with these and other insects, and so feared he wouldn't sleep. He gripped the bed-post, and tucked himself firmly under the crisp linen sheets, as if retreating into the safety of a finely-lined cage that would grant him protection.

In the midst of this anxiety, he thought he heard faint footsteps. He heard the wooden floorboards creak like the wheels of a carriage – regular, soft, then louder and louder – and allowed himself to imagine all manner of surprises these sounds might foretell. Given his troubled state of mind, he expected the surprise would be unwelcome. And so he put on the treasured spectacles he'd laid on the table by the bedside, in order to see better what was coming his direction, and to prepare himself for the worst.

He needn't have worried. When it came, the knock on the door was soft, and as the stiff latch opened, he saw Abigail standing before him, carrying with her a simple silver tray with which to offer him hot tea and biscuits. She greeted him with her captivating smile, dressed in a glossy nightgown of luxurious blue satin, loosely woven and loosely fitting. Never had a woman seemed more bewitching to him than she did now. Gareth returned the handsome smile with one of his own, and without any hesitancy, Abigail stepped inside and closed the door behind her, securing the rusty latch for good measure.

* *

The governor found everything to be in order at Fort Hamilton. Or at least, he found it to be much as he anticipated.

His report of this visit might as well have been copied out directly from the last dispatch he'd made several months before, given how little had changed since then. There was the usual indolence of the men, and the generalized untidiness about the place that, to his finicky eye, bordered on chaos. But the men had exceeded their quota of captives for the period, and so he was inclined to be forgiving. Given such a performance, he knew his masters in London certainly would be. Besides, as always, his brief visit wouldn't last long enough for him to see beyond the wispy veneer the men had erected, to the real, long-term damage the soldiers were slowly inflicting on the site.

There was nothing unusual on the return journey either. There was only the same hypnotic monotony and poor road conditions that would try the most tenacious of travelers. Several times his horse bucked, on passing by a slothful porcupine or on entering a ditch whose depth it had ill-judged. One soldier in the group had earned a censure for appearing to repeat within his earshot a much-repeated joke lampooning the reputedly lackluster skills of King George in satisfying his many putative mistresses. True or not, Governor Marsh reckoned that a clear if inoffensive show of discipline toward the troops was only ever a good thing.

His path, however, was soon slowed by an obstacle. Two young men were blocking the way with the spilled contents of the cart they were pulling. Rows and rows of freshly-cut logs for firewood were dribbling out onto the path as if in slow motion.

"What is it?" shouted the governor to his Fante attendant, who was out in front leading the escort. "Why have we stopped?" Seeing for himself the carnage on the roadside, he continued, "Tell them to hurry it up, won't you. Are these boys yours? Are they Fante?"

"No, Captain," he replied, though "captain" was hardly the correct way to address him. "Ashanti people. Come from Sehwi."

"The Fante's enemy, sir," said the recently admonished English soldier. "Never long without a skirmish or two. Sehwi, I think, is inland, about thirty miles west of here. The local chief and his people there, they serve the Dutch forces."

"I know where Sehwi is, you fool," he shot back. Still, the governor was astonished his guide could make out an enemy so easily, in the form of these unlucky young men. Not only their tribe, but the village from where they were likely to come, despite the similarities with his guide's physiognomy, comparable body markings and, to the governor's ear, the same language.

And it was there and then that it dawned on him how to solve the vexatious conundrum of the chief's disappeared son. For although the English couldn't definitively identify the boy, he'd suddenly worked out that one of their own kind would certainly be able to do so.

He hurried back to the fort, instructing his escort not to be restrained by any hitches in the road or by his troops' fatigue. And when at last he entered the main house, he raced to the dining room, where he found his wife and their visitor already seated at luncheon. Abigail was dressed quite conventionally, but he was startled to see the clerk dressed in his shirtsleeves, the pair laughing robustly, like schoolgirls sharing a closely-held secret.

"Listen," he said, aiming his short-winded comments directly at Gareth. "I know what it is we must do."

"Must do for *what?*"

"To get that boy William back, of course! I've had time to think about this, and the solution's become more than obvious to me. You'll kick yourself for not having thought of it first."

"I'm sure I will."

"Let's go ahead and get the other boy in here."

"Which one would that be?" asked Gareth, still reeling from seeing the governor returned, unannounced.

"The chief's rep. Name's Kwame, or some such. He's been coming here every full moon, his visits as irritating as all hell. He's been hounding us for months with his bluster and his threats."

"Can't you just *ignore* the boy?" chimed in Abigail.

"You know nothing of it, Abi."

"Really, Thomas, there's no need to be short with me."

Ignoring her remonstrations, he continued. "We'll bring him here and tell him what we know. We'll lay out the long list of extortionate terms demanded of us by this piddling plantation owner. Every last one of them."

"And what *then*? What good will come of that?"

"You and I, Bain," replied the governor, "we'll find a way to meet these demands. *All* of them. But as for identifying the boy, I'm going to suggest that we send someone. Someone from here who'll be able to positively identify him. Who can testify to it. I'm sure this Kwame can volunteer someone to go."

Governor Marsh paused for brief a moment. Long enough to cross the room, and to fill high his whiskey glass. Then, leaning over to the clerk, he added, "I'd venture to say, we might even get him to go himself."

## CHAPTER 14

The line between hope and despair, between exultation and grief, is often desperately thin. As thin, and as sinuous, as the sweeping line Kwame was drawing in the sand. He was outlining from memory, with the aid of a jagged tree branch, the broad contours of the Annamaboe coast, or at least as far as he'd known it. He was tracing the tight orbit, not more than a few miles long and fewer still wide, that marked the boundaries of his world. He was practicing so that, like the surveyor or the seasoned explorer, he could reproduce the outline at will – on another beach, in another land – now that the rigid confines of that orbit were poised to open up to him.

All of his young life, it had been as if he'd been trapped in the heart of a heavy mist: close-in he could see everything sharply, but farther ahead, as it was behind, things were more blurred. He'd always wondered what lay beyond that mist, and what kind of revelations, what manner of fortune, might govern his future. And like those great explorers, who sailed every year for mile upon unchartered mile, like the unflagging gulls swirling overhead, he was consumed by an irrepressible lust to wander and to know for himself the mysteries and the miracles of the world. And now, quite unexpectedly, that opportunity had come at last.

The patchy line he traced in the sand went only as far as Bogi Cove. At one time, he'd known all the landmarks along the way; every jetty and breakwater, the most fertile points where the fishermen would cast their nets, and where the riptides were most perilous. With their knives, he and William had once cut tiny notches into the side of their canoe, marking the number of times they'd taken that trip together. But any trace of that canoe had been swallowed up by the bottomless ocean; the bark on any tree where, with those same knives they'd carved their names, would slowly have begun to grow over. Any fortress of shells or column of pebbles they'd competed to construct would have long since collapsed, and with it, any record of their ever having been there except their memory of it. It had been so long now, Kwame began to doubt even that. He questioned the distances to the salt marsh, where the storm waves had wantonly cut a pathway that the boys had sometimes used as a shortcut. Did the arch of their favorite rock formation, the one that William said looked as if overnight it had sprouted intact from the depths of the hostile sea, have a level plateau or a rounded one? At the lagoon, was it the first wooden pier that had been struck by lightning, not once but twice, or was it the last one?

Memory, however, can be dogged. The passage of so much time might have obscured some of the landmarks, but it couldn't erase the more vivid recollections, the many delights, he'd known at the cove, for these had marked his childhood. And it wasn't just these surreptitious excursions, but it was the same for all of the jubilant times he'd spent with William. He was the one true friend who – until what Kwame had taken for an unforgivable betrayal, until his disappearance – had given him the gift of wonder. Until by his own hand he'd undone all that, or at least had allowed it to be undone.

Yet this morning, alone on the gusty beach, he was reminded too of his one binding conviction, of his one promise to the gods, made in this same place, to reverse that damage. And like a hero who invariably arrives just in time, it appeared as if that time was finally upon him.

But heroes, he knew, sometimes fail. Sometimes their victory in one arena can engender defeat in another. What if he'd agreed too quickly to the English plan? What if their unscrupulous merchants didn't respect that plan? They'd certainly not respected the arrangements for his friend, all those years ago, and now they had left him with little choice. He'd travel with them the thousands of miles across an ocean he knew to be voracious. He'd recognize William. He'd identify him for the authorities, and by his word set him free, just as by his silence he'd once condemned him. But would William recognize *him*? For Kwame had changed. He might have looked similar, he carried the same strong if lean form, but he wasn't the flighty boy he once had been. He'd become the shadow of a man, and if not completely extinguished, some of the light behind his eyes had dimmed.

He took in great, deep breaths of the briny air, as if to draw in more of everything about the place, from the smell of the sea spray to the unmistakable sound of the squally waves forever crashing on the shore. Soon he'd have to join the others, but first, still secluded from them, he'd nurse the wound of his new tattoo that was still uncomfortably sore. Yesterday, when the priest cut the pattern into his arm, he'd almost invited the pain. The agony of its application would make him prouder to carry it. Like Badu and William before him, wherever he might go he would bear these markings as a unique symbol of the tribe, and of his devotion to it.

It was all he could do not to pick at the wound with his fingers, so he sat with his hands tightly gripping the knobby branch he still held, before relinquishing it and placing his perspiring hands on his flushed face. He could see the throbbing veins of his hands. He could feel the muscles in his cheeks tighten and twitch. Slowly, like the closing of a plaited fan, he moved his fingers across his eyes until he could no longer see. Until there was nothing left but blackness, as if this so familiar land had disappeared before him already. It would take all the courage he could muster not to weep. He'd need to hold fast to that courage to get through the interminable anticipation of his departure.

He wouldn't have long to wait. Like those gulls whose flight he'd always envied, tomorrow he'd be leaving. But not for the kind of exploit he'd always imagined, or at all as he dreamed it to be. His leaving was not in the pursuit of some great adventure. It wasn't some momentous, epic enterprise. He wouldn't go, as William had anointed him, as a lionized ruler of the seas, but as a pawn in the endless game that the English and his own people were set on playing against each other. It was a game they'd been playing for a hundred years, and that none would ever win. That none ever could. As for his part in this hollow contest, too much had been lost already. There had been so many calamities along the way, it was little wonder the waiting was getting the better of him.

So when at last he came upon the ceremony in his honor at the sacred grove, already well underway, he sat slightly apart while the others rejoiced. Still, he knew his role. He knew what was expected of him. After all, he'd been acting out a role for months, that of the steely negotiator, of dutiful servant to the chief, and of confident, impassive messenger. He'd been no such thing. He'd allowed himself to be seduced by the role, by the regalia, and by the prestige it afforded. He'd been duped by the encouragement of others too. But in his quieter moments, Kwame knew his confidence was a pretense, constructed for the chief's benefit, and with a single purpose in mind: to secure William's return. He was only afraid that, now that this purpose was on the point of being realized, his confidence and his faith might fall apart or wash away, like the line in the sand he'd been drawing earlier.

All afternoon he'd play along, while the children reveled in the pageantry and the women formed a chorus and sang songs. They were traditional songs of rejoicing and praise that lifted them all. For a time, he sang along with them, but his heart was never really in it. No one had noticed his detachment, or the mournfulness in his soft eyes. No one really tried. They paid him little attention, though ostensibly he was the sole object of all the bustle and conviviality.

And a bustle it was. Today's grand events had been going on since midday. By now the women's chorus was accompanied by the men's bellowing percussion, and by costumed men who shook their gourds filled with seeds or with beads. They vigorously hit their tenor-drums and talking-drums with open palms, and rang their bells of all shapes and sizes. The children, with no instruments to call their own, clapped their hands together. When a group of young girls began their dance of the antelope – an almost forgotten dance to mimic the animal's sacrifice, and to signify the restoration to health of the spirits – a frenzy of jubilation and of laughter broke out. It was as if the health not just of the spirits, but of everyone in the chief's villages, had suddenly been renewed, like a siege or a curse had been lifted. As if a terrible, battering storm had finally subsided.

Kwame watched the peculiar dance with awe. He watched as the pace quickened, unsure if the drummers were leading the dancers to greater speed, or if it was the other way around, marveling either way at the spontaneous communication between them. Those on the outside of the circle were just as swept up by the excitement as those on the inside; they were intoxicated by it, swaying back and forth, waiting impatiently for their turn to partake. Adwoa went so far as to tap Chief Kurentsi on the shoulder with the traditional red sash, signaling that he should join the ring as the next participant. To everyone's surprise, he did just that. He entered enthusiastically, swinging his arms, capering about as lively as any of the others, attempting the complex footwork in keeping with the increasingly fast drumming, as if he'd been doing this routinely. It was as if something dormant in him had been awakened. He was cheerful in a way few could remember seeing him, and he didn't seem to mind who knew it.

The chief's participation in the dance was the clearest of indications of the unusually celebratory mood surrounding Kwame's imminent journey. But everyone, including Kwame, knew that he was not the real intended object of their merriment; it wasn't his departure they were marking, but the inevitable recovery of William that this trip presaged. If Governor Marsh still harbored doubts about the consummation of this mission, if Gareth Bain still agonized over its outcome, few others did so. The oracle foretold of its success. The omens were clear enough. The people latched on to his liberation. They divined his homecoming. And they wouldn't miss any chance to herald it.

Kwame couldn't see any of this. He couldn't allow himself to share in the joys of the day. And when he stepped away from the revelers, from the stragglers who lingered in the circle, hardly anyone noticed.

He walked alone up the sharp bluff, to the open-air schoolroom at the edge of the chief's compound. The sparse room had long lain idle. Dusty, covered in ropy spider webs, the chalkboard still showed faint, illegible vestiges of the cursive script and simple arithmetic he and William had been taught there. He made straight for the disused cupboard, and rummaged through the cluttered stacks of papers until he found what he was looking for: the short pamphlet issued by His Majesty's Service at Sea that, years before, they'd traded an English merchant for a pouch full of cashew nuts, to feed their obsession for all things maritime. It was a tract they'd consulted for hour upon truant hour on the hillside above the port, as they watched the imposing tide of foreign ships coming into the harbor.

Yellowed, dog-eared, he knew the pamphlet well enough to know that it wouldn't be especially useful to him, but at least it could occupy him for a time. So he buried himself in it, in the rules and regulations of the merchant trade, reminding himself of the various ranks and ratings of the men he might encounter on-board, and the bemusing, incomprehensible nicknames they'd invented for each one of them. He meditated over the long catalogue of punishments that might be meted out to the crew – the flogging with knotted ropes, canings, and worse – for a cook who spoiled a meal, for calling someone a liar in the mess or, worst of all, for stealing from another crewmate. He carefully studied one of the more graphic illustrations of those sanctions, of an offender tied up for dozing on watch, with his hands high above his head and a bucket of sea-water being poured down his sleeves. There was a whole section on why whistling was prohibited, and why it would also be punished, since it could too easily be confused with the boatswain's call.

There was hardly any risk of his falling afoul of any of these rules, and none more so than the last one. He didn't know how to whistle, and had always failed miserably when William encouraged him to try. He tried again now, but still it was no use. The sound that emerged was as dissonant as the sharpening of a knife-edge on a wet stone-wheel.

Eukobah, who passed near to the schoolroom as she crossed the adjacent yard, spied him doing this. She overheard his feeble attempts at whistling, and mistook them for an expression of happiness, and so she smiled her delicate smile. To her, it was affirmation of the gentle words she'd offered him, when she'd found him at his lowest point after Esi's fall: that however dark the sky, there would always be a morning. So had morning finally come for him? Eukobah was certain it had, and for this, she was truly thankful.

What was undeniable to her was that he'd finally proved himself useful. He was demonstrating his genuine value to the tribe. As testament to this, at the ceremony she'd seen the chief present him with an amulet to wear on his belt – a small, conical-shaped, scowling mask, with bones, teeth and seeds encrusted in the wood – to ward off harm and illness. The chief had held Kwame's hand in his own long enough to signify gratitude. The message of forgiveness, of acceptance, was unequivocal.

All of this attention, this adulation, was foreign to Kwame, and it wasn't entirely welcome, as he was still tormented by fearful thoughts. By the notion that all of this was his fault in the first place, and by the knowledge that he'd forsworn the friend who'd shown him such affection and such sympathy. William was likely still in chains a world away, almost as if it had been by Kwame's own hands; he'd had the power to stop it, and he had chosen otherwise. It had been an error of supreme selfishness, or of foolishness, that had come to define him. It had haunted his waking hours since, as it had haunted his sleep, and he had no one to blame but himself for all that followed.

But the trouble was much greater than that, since Kwame was also haunted by the private recognition that the hopeful morning Eukobah promised would likely never come to pass, and that only he and the chief, the governor and the visiting clerk, knew why. That he wasn't going on this long journey as a hero, and that he wasn't going only to identify William. And despite the amulet strapped to his belt, little could shield him from what was in store.

For he had to abide strict adherence to the terms – all of the terms – of the deal. They were negotiations he'd led, and in which he'd represented the tribe well. Only yesterday he'd reviewed with the chief the lengthy demands of the plantation owner, and the plan he and the governor had hastily agreed, that included a huge sum of money to be paid from the king's waning exchequer, and that was many times what the owner would have paid for William four years prior.

The chief was pleased the bargain would cost the English so dearly, as if it were an indication of William's worth. After all, there was practically no price too high for them to pay for the return of his son. But more than that, the price was unmistakably rich enough to signal the chief's continued sovereignty over his intractable adversary. No tariff was too steep to prove or flaunt his paramount status. In return, none of the concessions on his part seemed undue. Not even the final, cold-blooded terms of the agreement.

In addition to the funds, the uncompromising plantation owner had called for a swap. He demanded in William's place a strong, similarly capable man of equivalent value. Though there would be a wealth of these to choose from, he also required a slave who could read and write and, not least, one who could communicate in English. He needed someone to serve, as William had done, as a broker between his slaves and his overseers, and who could help to ensure that the fragile peace between them continued. And in Annamaboe there was only one person who could fulfill these criteria: Kwame himself.

With the chief's consent, he was to be the linchpin of the deal he had himself negotiated. As the triumphant convoy prepared to leave Bridgetown for London with a liberated William aboard, he'd stay behind – as compensation and as ransom. It was a final act of sacrifice, and an act of contrition, after which the chief might pardon his carelessness and the gods might forgive his trespass. It was an act by which William might forgive him, too. And by which, as he took up the sorrowful position his true friend had vacated, he might just come to forgive himself.

With the sailor's pamphlet now tucked firmly in his sleeve, Kwame made his way down the hill from the chief's compound. He walked past the throng of well-wishers and through the village, on the dusty paths he knew by heart, and straight to the harbor. Across the row of busy quays, he saw the massive English ship, and was staggered by the grandeur of it. For all the time he'd spent admiring these ships from afar, he'd not once boarded one. What he saw when he climbed onto the vessel astounded him. There were mountains of rigging. Sails, still folded, stood taller than he was. There was a bewildering kaleidoscope of cargo, being loaded and unloaded with military precision.

The smells of tobacco and sweat overwhelmed him, as did the booming sounding of the bells as, for the last time that evening, the half-hour glass was turned.

He sat alone, unobserved and undisturbed, for hours, as around him the daylight waned. And as the moon rose higher and higher over the shimmering horizon, he admired the gentle light it cast, without the usual hindrance of the campfires and torches in his village to oppose it. All the while he wondered when the crew would come for him. At what point would they cuff the chains on his wrists, and drag him below. He knew they would come; he didn't fear it. Now that the evening tide had risen and the anchor had been hoisted, he wanted only to stay on deck a little longer to savor the soft bands of that moonlight, in hues of pale white and ashen grey, that streamed across the landscape, and that broke through the high clouds like ghostly braids.

And he wanted one more look. One last, close look at that coastline, for any tracing in sand or on a map he might one day be called on to make of this place. It was a place that, when asked, and despite all his troubles and disappointments there, he'd say was a paradise.

He stroked the talisman on his belt, despite himself, as he had little faith in its power to protect him. Even as he did so, he could feel the sky closing in. Like the line between hope and despair, the contours of the shore were becoming thin and shadowy. Until slowly the faint coastline, until the sky itself, faded into darkness.

# AFTERWORD:
# THE LIFE AND TIMES OF
# WILLIAM ANSAH SESSARAKOO

# TIMELINE OF EVENTS

| | |
|---|---|
| c.1725–30 | Born son of Eno Baise Kurentsi, a chief of the Fante people, known to the English as John Corrantee. |
| 1744 | Sent to England to learn about business. Reaches Barbados and is sold into slavery. |
| 1744–48 | News of his fate causes a diplomatic incident, with Corrantee threatening to cease trade with Britain. |
| 1748 | Royal African Company secures his freedom. |
| 1749 | Arrives in London, received by George Montagu Dunk, second Earl of Halifax. |
| Feb. 1749 | Attends a performance of *Oroonoko*; his story is told in *Gentleman's Magazine*. |
| July/Aug. 1749 | 'The African Prince' appears in *Gentleman's Magazine*. |
| Nov. 1749 | Baptized into the Anglican faith. |
| Late 1749 | Portrait painted in oils by Gabriel Mathias. |
| Aug. 1750 | Leaves for Africa on-board *HMS Surprize*. |
| Nov. 1750 | Meets John Newton, then a slave trader, later to be a noted abolitionist and author of "Amazing Grace." |
| April 1751 | Arrives home. Hired as a clerk by the Company of Merchants Trading to Africa. |
| April 30, 1770 | Dies of unknown causes. |

# THE LIFE AND TIMES OF
# WILLIAM ANSAH SESSARAKOO

*by Professor Nicholas Cheeseman*
*Director, Centre for African Studies*
*Oxford University*

Few hard facts are known about the early life of William Ansah Sessarakoo, but it seems likely that he was born at Annamaboe (present-day Anomabu, in southern Ghana) in the late 1720s to Eno Baise Kurentsi, a chief of the Fante people – known as John Bannishee Corrantee to the English – and Eukobah, daughter of Ansah Sessarakoo, king of Aquamboo. As a young man he befriended British traders working on the Gold Coast who, because of his amiable nature and "graceful Deportment," nicknamed him "Cupid."

Sessarakoo's curiosity and early education in the English language from the merchants and others at Annamaboe encouraged his father to send him to Britain to receive further education when he was eighteen or nineteen years old, a crucial turning point in his life.

The decision to send Sessarakoo to Britain was not the selfless act it might first appear, and needs to be understood in the context of heated international competition for African resources at the time. Corrantee was one of the primary gold and slave traders on the Gold Coast, and well appreciated the value of being able to play different European powers off against each other. He had already sent one of his sons, known to the British as Lewis Banishee, to France in order to strengthen his ties with French traders. He was therefore favorably disposed to the suggestion of an unnamed English captain (probably David Bruce Crichton) to take Sessarakoo to Britain to further develop his relationship with the British, so as to better benefit from the rivalry between the two great European powers. Corrantee's best laid plans, however, went awry when the captain betrayed his trust and sold Sessarakoo into slavery when the ship reached Barbados in 1744.

This is not a unique story; there is evidence that a growing number of "noble Africans" headed for Britain in search of education during the eighteenth century. This reflected broader trends on the Gold Coast, where the children of local notables were often encouraged by their parents to learn English from merchants and traders so that the family could take full advantage of new opportunities generated by European trade. While some made it, a considerable number shared Sessarakoo's misfortune, including figures who would also go on to achieve similar notoriety, such as Job Ben Soloman, a Muslim whose memoirs became one of the first slave narratives.

The enslavement of Sessarakoo came to light when the ship reached Barbados. Fortunately for him, the captain passed away en route before the ship returned to Britain, which freed other members of the crew to tell the authorities about the incident in some detail.

The news of Sessarakoo's enslavement sparked a diplomatic incident. By threatening to cease trading with

Britain, Corrantee was able to force the Royal African Company to pay the ransom required to bring Sessarakoo back to Britain. The influence that Corrantee was able to exert in favor of his son is telling, because it demonstrates that African traders in strategically important locations such as Annamaboe – a key link in the Atlantic slave trade, described by the Royal African Company as "the key to whole trade of the Gold Coast" – could wield a significant amount of agency and power. Indeed, British officials grumbled at their lack of control over Corrantee, and complained about the fact that he continued to trade heavily with other nations despite British efforts to rescue his son and to take care of him.

Sessarakoo's experiences in Britain, and what we know of him today, owed much to the efforts of George Montagu Dunk, second Earl of Halifax. Dunk was a colorful character who became known as the "father of the colonies" as a result of his success in extending American commerce. He is now perhaps best remembered as the man who aided the foundation of Nova Scotia, in return for which its capital – Halifax – was named after him. In 1748, Dunk was made the President of the Board of Trade and Plantations, a position he held until 1761, in which capacity he took a special interest in the lives of a number of "royal Africans." When William Ansah Sessarakoo arrived in London society in 1749, Dunk received him and became his patron.

It was at this point that the second stage of William Ansah Sessarakoo's life began to unfold. He was introduced to King George II, attended a session at the House of Lords, and began to appear at London theaters. We know that he attended the tragedy of *Oroonoko* at Covent Garden, powdered and wigged like an English gentleman, where he is said to have received a loud round of applause from the audience and to have responded with a genteel bow. The play – which features the abuse of power by a ship captain similar to that which the young African suffered himself – was said to have rendered him overcome with emotion, and he may even have run out of the theater, leaving a strong and sympathetic impression on the British audience. Perhaps as a result of this traumatic experience, Sessarakoo subsequently became known for watching only comedies at the Theatre Royal.

Later that same year the first article about Sessarakoo was published in *Gentleman's Magazine.* The piece provided possibly the most complete and verifiable contemporary account of his arrival and reception in England, including the details about his capture and subsequent release. It was also notable for laying down the blueprint for most subsequent accounts of his life. Christened the "Prince of Annamaboe" by a fascinated press, Sessarakoo became something of a fixture in a number of London-based periodicals such as the *London Intelligencier,* which repeated and embellished this narrative. Others, such as the *London Gazeteer,* offered their own twists on the tale, claiming for instance that Sessarakoo received instruction in dancing and other popular English pursuits. The strength of public interest in the story is confirmed by Horace Walpole, who in March 1749 wrote to Horace Mann, then resident in Italy, that: "There are two black princes of Anamaboe here, who are in fashion at all the assemblies, of whom I scarcely know any particulars, though their story is very like Oroonoko's; all the women know it—and ten times more than belongs to it."

During this period, Sessarakoo's education and integration into English life owed much to Dunk's patronage. The first article about Sessarakoo and his fellow African notables in *Gentleman's Magazine* reported that Dunk had given orders that they should be clothed and educated "in a very genteel manner." One consequence of this was that an Anglican Bishop, Thomas Sherlock, appointed the reader of Temple Church in London, was to instruct Sessarakoo in the "principles of Christian religion." Dunk's influence was also central to the growth of Sessarakoo's fame, because some of the authors whose stories and poems raised awareness of him did so because they hoped to attract Dunk's patronage. For example, William Dodd, who immortalized Sessarakoo in the poem "The African Prince," published in two parts in 1749, dedicated his work not to the African prince, but to the Earl of Halifax.

Dodd's poem is instructive, because it highlights the internal tension present in many accounts of Sessarakoo, which cannot decide between portraying him as a royal savage whose particular breeding engenders him with an innate nobility, or as a lost soul saved by his exposure to upper class English culture, which enabled him to be elevated above the level of other Africans. This tension is important, because it reflects a broader set of debates around issues of race and rights in Britain at the time. Over the course of twenty years, discourses that had previously implied that only a small number of Africans could ever approach civilized status – the exception that proved the rule – gradually gave way to concerns about the need to save all African souls, and a desire to undertake "civilizing missions" as part of the "white man's burden." In many ways, it could be argued that Sessarakoo occupied a middle point in the transformation of this debate.

Public and intellectual interest in Sessarakoo also reflected an ongoing fascination throughout the eighteenth century with the trope of the "visiting foreigner," who was valued as an exotic figure, much celebrated in literature and the popular press. Periodicals such as the *Gentleman's Magazine* contain frequent references to "Moorish Kings" and figures such as "an Arab Sheikh of Zanzibar." Further evidence of the broader resonance of these stories can be seen in the longstanding popularity of the *Oroonoko* story, which was first published in a 1688 novella of the same name by Aphra Behn and later transferred to the stage by Thomas Southerne. *Oroonoko* told the tale of the titular "Royal Slave" sold into slavery in Suriname, the West Indies, before (in Southerne's version) returning free and triumphant to his African home. The parallels between the story of Oroonoko and the life of Sessarakoo were not lost on contemporaries – not least because one of Sessarakoo's first recorded outings in Britain was to see the play – and this particular metaphor recurred both during and after Sessarakoo's death, as anti-slavery campaigners began to make the case that Africans, too, could benefit from exposure to European civilization.

The extent and the significance of Sessarakoo's entry into British society should not, however, be exaggerated. Some rejected his "princely" status, and he was always viewed as something of a curiosity. But the presence of figures such as Sessarakoo was nonetheless important, because their "improvement" in Britain was taken by proponents of the "civilizing mission" as evidence of the truth of their cause. The ultimate proof of Sessarakoo's own capacity for "improvement" was provided by two events in late 1749. First, his religious education lessons went so well that on 30 November he was baptized into the Church of England. Second, in the final months of the year, interest in Sessarakoo, and his reputation for graceful behavior, was sufficient to merit a portrait in oils by noted Court-painter

Gabriel Mathias, an engraved copy of which appeared in the June 1750 issue of *Gentleman's Magazine*, and which today sits in the National Portrait Gallery in London.

But no sooner had Sessarakoo started to make his mark on England than he left to return to Africa. On 14 August 1750, he set sail for home on board *HMS Surprize*, under the watchful eye of Captain Patrick Baird. Sessarakoo's journey was an eventful one, in part because Baird stopped to inspect British factories along the African Coast on the way, and on 24 November he met John Newton off the coast of Sierra Leone. At the time Newton was a well-known slave trader, but later became a noted abolitionist who also made his name by writing the hymn "Amazing Grace." Newton recorded being impressed with Sessarakoo in his diary, noting that he was the "master of a great deal of solid sense and a politeness of behaviour I seldom meet with in any of our own complexion hereabouts." Statements such as this suggest that the experience of meeting educated royal Africans like Sessarakoo played an important role in changing the attitudes of men like Newton to slavery.

Just over four months after he set sail from the U.K., Sessarakoo arrived home. He was quickly hired as a clerk by John Roberts, governor-in-chief of all the British factories on the Gold Coast maintained by the Company of Merchants Trading to Africa (successor to the Royal African Company), who was keen to maintain good ties with Corrantee. The extent of Sessarakoo's British assimilation, and the emerging ambiguities in British attitudes to race and slavery, can be seen from the fact that his employment was listed with European staff rather than with African staff, albeit with the qualification "black." His father, pleased to have his son back home, wrote a letter of thanks to the Board of Admiralty that was published in the *London*

*Evening Post*, demonstrating the continued interest in the "Prince of Annamaboe."

From this point on, however, far fewer details of Sessarakoo's life are known, and he died of unknown causes on 30 April 1770.

Yet one of the most interesting things about William Ansah Sessarakoo is his remarkable afterlife. As with many other African notables who came to grief during the slave trade, Sessarakoo's story was taken up by people with a specific political vision and cause. This is most clearly the case with *The Royal African: Or Memoirs of the Young Prince of Annamaboe*, an anonymous account of Sessarakoo's life styled as a memoir. *The Royal African* was so popular that it went through three editions, but actually sheds relatively little light on Sessarakoo's real life and times. Rather, it functions more as a piece of political propaganda, suggesting that Sessarakoo owed his release to the good nature of the merchants of the Royal African Company, who felt his enslavement was at odds with their understanding of liberty and justice.

Of course, the idea that Royal Africans were liberated by "the natural Candour and Generosity of a true English Soul" is impossible to square with the fact that every year at least 20,000 slaves were carried from Africa to the West Indies. Yet as problematic as this depiction is, it also points to the way in which those who sought to call into question the morality of slavery adopted accounts of lives such as Sessarakoo's for their own purposes. In the 1770s and 1780s, some of Britain's best known romantic writers such as William Blake, Samuel Taylor Coleridge, and William Wordsworth began to write about – and bemoan – the fate of "noble African slaves." When later campaigners came to describe the brutality of the slave trade, and to reject the idea of Africans as a sub-human race of savages, they made much of the fact that figures such as William Ansah Sessarakoo had already demonstrated their ability to integrate into British life.